LEAD

Elise Noble

Published by Undercover Publishing Limited

ISBN: 978-1-910954-98-0

Edited by Amanda Ann Larson

www.undercover-publishing.com

www.elise-noble.com

CHAPTER 1 - IMOGEN

"SO LET ME get this straight," Stefanie said to me as I sank onto one of the white leather couches in her living room. "Jean-Luc invited you out for dinner and then expected you to entertain his girlfriend?"

"Well, technically it wasn't dinner. It was a cooking contest, and we got to sample some of the dishes."

Stef rolled her eyes. "Imogen, that's not the point I was trying to make."

I knew that. Of course I knew that. But trying to avoid the real issue—that Jean-Luc had invited me on what I thought was a date but which turned out to be definitely not a date made my disappointment easier to bear. Okay, it didn't, but I had to try, right?

Probably I should start at the beginning, shouldn't I? My name's Imogen Blair, and I'm unlucky in love. And lust, and like, and anything else that might happen with a man. Take the last guy I dated, for instance. Three weeks in, he let slip that he had two kids back in Utah by his ex-girlfriend that he'd just...abandoned. Long-term prospects? Zero. Before that mistake, I'd gone out with a guy whose idea of showing a girl a good time was to take her to his mom's house for a home-cooked dinner, nod approvingly as Mom interrogated her, then try for third base while they watched a Disney movie in the basement with Mom's footsteps clomping overhead. Oh, and in a spectacular error of judgement a year ago, I'd gotten cheated on by a suspected drug dealer.

Bad enough, but not as awful as the two years I spent as a call girl. Life had led me down a dark path until that point, and when you're desperate for money, and your life's in the toilet, and you've watched Pretty Woman more times than was healthy, you'll do some really, really stupid things. Eventually, I came to my senses and realised a wealthy businessman wasn't going to buy me jewellery and take me to the opera, so I retired from that "career," but it turned out that the assholes willing to hook up with a barista or a waitress or a nail technician weren't any better.

By now, you're most likely wondering why I bothered dating at all, and believe me, I'd asked myself the same question many times. I guess I just didn't want to give up on my dream. Two of my friends had recently gotten engaged, and seeing how happy they were gave me hope. Hope that I'd find a man to share my life with. Hope that I could be one half of something special. Hope that I'd get the big white wedding I'd been daydreaming about since I was a little girl.

And then there was Jean-Luc Fortier, a pastry chef who worked at Rhodium, one of the restaurants part-owned by Stef's fiancé, Oliver. I'd worked there for a while too until I started my own nail salon, and even now I still did the occasional evening shift when things were slow at the Nailed It, which had the added bonus of letting me spend time with Monsieur Fortier. The perfect man—soft brown eyes, long, elegant fingers, and a French accent that made me shiver. Kind, sexy, and generous with the free cakes and pastries. So what was the problem? Well, he'd friend-zoned me from the moment he first showed me around the restaurant, and I'd been trying to clamber out of that box ever since.

Setbacks such as Jean-Luc casually mentioning his latest girlfriend left me depressed, even if his girlfriends never seemed to last for long, and that was when I did dumb things like going speed-dating or hooking up with a bartender who expected me to bow down to his four-inch dick. *Stupid, stupid Imogen.* After this latest debacle, with my judgement so badly impaired, I'd have to be careful not to sleep with a serial killer like Stef accidentally did.

"Have you got any wine?" I asked. I couldn't go out with an idiot if I was unconscious, could I?

Stef regarded me doubtfully. "Are you sure that's the answer?"

"I'm not sure about anything anymore."

Roxy glided across the room, so elegant and six inches taller than me. "No wine. You need to find a better man than Jean-Luc. One who doesn't send mixed signals then invite you along as the third-wheel."

"It was probably my fault for misunderstanding."

"What exactly did he say?"

"That he was taking part in La Parade des Chefs and would I like to come and watch?"

"No mention of a girlfriend?"

"Nope."

"Are you sure?" Stef asked.

"I think I'd remember."

"That's... That's so...so *rude.*"

"Perhaps I should've asked? And besides, Jean-Luc doesn't know how I feel."

"Stop making excuses for him. From this moment

on, it's no more Jean-Luc. He's not good for you, the way he keeps messing you around. We can get our cakes from somewhere else."

"Claude's patisserie has a good selection," Roxy said. "That's where Gideon always goes."

Gideon was her ridiculously rich, obscenely hot fiancé, a man way out of my league but perfectly suited to Roxy, a girl who managed to be kind, generous, and beautiful all at the same time. And smart. Did I mention smart? Roxy was training as a neurosurgeon at Richmond General. But today, there was a flaw in her plan.

"I can't avoid Jean-Luc. He qualified for the final in two weeks time, and I promised I'd go."

"With the girlfriend?"

"What was I supposed to say? I'd have looked horrible if I'd refused."

"Is she nice?"

"Marelaine? No, she's the most self-centred woman I've ever met." And she was a model, a Brazilian version of Roxy in terms of looks, but if Marelaine had any redeeming qualities, I'd yet to find them. She definitely wasn't the right girl for Jean-Luc. He deserved better. "And her voice is like fingernails on a blackboard."

"So cancel," Roxy said. "You don't need her in your life."

"Jean-Luc asked me to do her nails tomorrow, and I accidentally agreed."

"Accidentally?"

"He smiled at me."

"Is she paying you for the manicure?"

Of course not. I bit my lip, embarrassed because Stef and Roxy wouldn't let themselves get walked all over like that.

"Apparently, she's an influencer on Instagram, and she'll share a post for the salon."

"Share a post?" Stef shook her head and blew out a long breath, but then she giggled.

"What's so funny?"

"This. Jean-Luc's such an asshole sometimes. I mean, how can he not have noticed that you want to push him back on the counter and lick whipped cream off his naked body? You know what we should do? Find you a much hotter guy and then you can parade him in front of Jean-Luc and see how he likes it."

"Reverse psychology?" Roxy said. "That might work. Make it clear to him what he's losing. But is it fair on the guy? Using him to get revenge on Jean-Luc?"

"The main point of this exercise is that Imogen could meet a man who's even *better* than Jean-Luc. That way, she'll realise what she's missing, and she'll be so busy having fun with her new beau, she won't even remember Jean-Luc's name."

Did I get any say in this? Stef's plan had "disaster" written all over it, and I hadn't even confessed the worst part yet, probably because I'd been in denial over my own stupidity. I buried my head in my hands.

"Uh..."

"What?" Stef asked. "What's wrong?"

"The hot guy? I only have two weeks to find him."

"Why? Imogen, what did you do?"

"When Jean-Luc invited me to the second challenge, I lost my mind and asked if I could bring my boyfriend along too."

I just snapped, okay? After two years of pining over Jean-Luc, the green-eyed monster came out in full force. And unless I was mistaken, there'd been a vague expression of shock on his face when I mentioned bringing a significant other. A slight widening of his eyes followed by a sideways glance at Marelaine. She'd looked surprised too, although perhaps that was because she couldn't imagine how a girl like me could possibly attract a man.

"And what did he say?" Stef asked.

"That he'd arrange another ticket." Followed by a nonchalant shrug that I wanted to believe was him trying to deal with my revelation.

"Then we definitely need to find you a date. I wonder if Oliver's got any hot attorney friends."

Yes, Stef had landed an attorney. A superstar attorney with an unrivalled record for winning and actual groupies who followed him to court and tossed underwear at him whenever he gave a press conference. I also knew from Stef's tipsy confessions that Oliver had a filthy streak as wide as the Atlantic, but the best part was that he was an excellent dad to their daughter, Abigail.

When it came to men, Roxy had gotten platinum, Stef scored gold, and I ended up with lead—dull, cheap, and poisonous if you got too close. With my biological clock ticking away, I'd have happily settled for silver or bronze, but even those seemed way out of my reach.

"Can you ask him?"

"As soon as he gets home. How about a paralegal? Would you consider a paralegal?"

"I'd settle for the janitor if he looked good in jeans and knew how to string a sentence together."

"Gideon might know someone," Roxy offered. "Although he usually hangs out with politicians."

I considered that for a second, but only for a second. I drew the line at politicians. In my days at the escort agency, Rubies are a Man's Best Friend, they were the worst kind of client—arrogant, entitled, and stingy. They never wanted to pay the full price, and they'd quibble over the extras. Like we were supposed to throw in a free blow job just because they'd managed to tell lies convincingly enough to get elected to public office.

"Can we skip the politicians? And the property developers too." One of those had almost been Stef's downfall. "Call me overcautious, but I'd rather avoid anyone with ready-made holes for burying my body should a date go fatally wrong."

"Statistically speaking—" Roxy started.

"I don't want to be a statistic. I've spent enough time hanging out around you guys and Blackwood that I just want a nice, normal guy who doesn't want to save the world or destroy it either."

By Blackwood, I meant Blackwood Security, a security and investigation firm based in Richmond and Oliver's main client. The whole firm seemed to be staffed by the love children of Wonder Woman and Superman, with the offspring of Thor and Charlie's Angels thrown in for good measure. Once, I'd have gone for the superhero, but I'd heard enough tales from Stef and Roxy about brushes with death and the havoc wreaked by bad guys that I'd changed my mind. If I finally ended up with the right man, I didn't want to sit at home alone in the evenings wondering whether he'd return on foot or in a body bag. Which was another reason Jean-Luc was perfect. How much harm could he come to in a kitchen? Sure, he nicked his fingers with a knife occasionally, but that wasn't life-threatening. I just needed to get him to see me as girlfriend material. That was my biggest hurdle.

Which reminded me—I needed to get my hair highlighted again. Jean-Luc had complimented me last time I had it done. He always noticed little things like that.

"So no politicians, no real estate developers, no Blackwood men," Roxy said. "How about cops? Men in uniform?"

"No cops and no military." They were just Blackwood lite.

"A fireman?" Stef asked. "A doctor?"

"I guess those would be okay. Bad guys don't usually shoot at firemen and doctors."

I'd been out with a doctor a couple of times, one I'd met when Stef got hit by a car and ended up in the hospital. He'd been nice, but I'd had my doubts over whether he was the one, and then he got a new job in Pennsylvania and that was the end of that. He'd refused to stay in Virginia—I wasn't the kind of girl a man rearranged his life for—and although he suggested I go with him, there was no way I'd ever move to Pittsburgh. Pittsburgh was too close to Cleveland for comfort.

"Roxy?" Stef said. "You work in a hospital. Who's available?"

"It's tricky—most of the good ones are married. A new intern just started, but I'm ninety percent sure he's gay. I'll check. Someone'll know for definite."

Stef bit the corner of her lip, thinking. "Even if he's gay, couldn't he just pretend for a day? You know, until the cooking competition's over?"

"We're supposed to be finding Imogen a life partner

here."

"What if that's Jean-Luc?" I asked.

"What if it isn't?"

Stef sided with Roxy. "I'll call Oliver and get a list of the single men at Rhodes, Holden and Maxwell." She patted me on the shoulder. "Don't worry; we'll find somebody in time."

This was what my love life had been reduced to— my two best friends calling around in search of a man who wasn't either married or gay. If reincarnation existed, next time I'd come back as a nun.

CHAPTER 2 - IMOGEN

"HOW ABOUT THIS one?" I suggested to Marelaine, holding up a bottle of Laguna Dreams nail polish. "The blue would match your eyes."

Although I swore they glowed red occasionally as the fires of hell glimmered through. So far, she'd insulted the decor in Nailed It ("Did you get the furniture from a discount store?"), my outfit ("The top doesn't do much for you, chica. You need a good support bra."), and my accent ("Where did you grow up? Detroit? Did you get shot at often?"), plus she'd rejected every single shade of polish I'd shown her. If she wasn't careful, she'd be wearing a bottle of Rainbow Shimmer Top Coat as a butt plug.

"I always think blue's so juvenile, don't you?"

Can you guess what colour my nails were?

If the salon had been empty, I'd have been tempted to give her a few choice words and kick her scrawny behind out the door, but my two assistants, Lisa and Charlene, both had clients, and my next appointment was waiting on the pale-grey leather couch by the door. No, diplomacy would have to win today, even if I cracked a tooth keeping my mouth shut.

What the hell did Jean-Luc see in this bitch? She might have been pretty on the outside, but she had an ugly soul. Unfortunately, he did have a tendency to get blinded by aesthetics—every man had a flaw or two, and that was Jean-Luc's biggest.

"Then how about a French manicure? That'll emphasise your natural beauty."

She nodded and huffed as if she was the one doing me the favour by allowing me to touch her talons. I'd wanted to file them shorter—better to stir her cauldron with—but she insisted on keeping them far too long to be practical. The logistics puzzled me. I mean, how did she wipe her ass with those claws?

I worked in blessed silence, willing myself not to smudge anything because that would undoubtedly lead to grumbling and she'd probably report my incompetence back to Jean-Luc too. Why did I let people like her make me feel so inferior? Just because she glided through life on five-inch pumps, looking down on the rest of us, didn't mean I was any less of a person.

As a teenager, I'd been first runner-up in the Junior Miss Cleveland pageant, but my former job and endless dating disasters had chipped away at my self-confidence until I second-guessed myself on everything. I'd read enough self-help books to know I did it, but changing my ways was a whole other problem.

We always have at least one reason to smile.

The framed quote above Marelaine's head had been hung there by Bradley, the interior designer Stef had co-opted to fit out the place, and most days, I could think of plenty of reasons to be happy. I loved my job. Opening a nail salon had been my dream for years, and I finally had the freedom of being my own boss.

Cheer up, Imogen.

I pictured Marelaine tripping over on the runway. There, now I felt better.

"All done. Just be careful not to touch them until the polish is completely dry. You're welcome to wait in the reception area if you want."

"Do those sofas have proper lumbar support?"

Thankfully my next client, Debra, appeared beside me before I could wrap my fingers around Marelaine's slender throat.

"The sofas are a bit lumpy," Debra said. "Perhaps you'd rather leave?"

"I'll need a cab," Marelaine told me. "Can you do my nails again in a couple of weeks?"

"I'm afraid I'm fully booked."

Screw her Instagram post. No amount of advertising was worth the stress of having to deal with Marelaine.

"Really?"

"Yes. I, uh, I'm taking some time off because my boyfriend and I are getting a puppy."

"A puppy?"

"Yes. Like a baby dog."

Oh, hell. What was I even saying? Obviously complete gibberish was spewing from my mouth because even Debra was looking at me strangely.

"What kind of puppy?" Marelaine asked. "My brother has a purebred Schnoodle."

Debra snorted. "What the heck is that?"

"A Schnauzer crossed with a Poodle."

"If it's a cross, how is it a purebred?"

Marelaine looked at Debra as if she was too stupid to be let out alone, then turned to me with an exaggerated roll of her eyes.

"Are you going to call that cab?"

With pleasure. I'd even shove her into it with my foot if it would help.

Debra managed to keep a straight face until Marelaine teetered out of the door on her obscenely high pumps, tossing a curtain of ebony hair behind her.

"What a bitch. You're really getting a puppy?"

"I wish. Not when I live in a fourth-floor apartment and work all day."

"Aw, puppies are cute. You could train it to sit by the door and growl at women like her. Or your boyfriend could help to take care of it." She gave me a nudge. "You sly little minx. Why didn't you tell me you were seeing somebody?"

Debra was a sweetheart, more of a friend now than a client, and as a rich banker's wife who got easily bored, she'd quite happily chat from dawn till dusk. If I didn't have an appointment right after hers, we often went out for coffee or lunch. She always paid, and I always felt guilty, but she insisted a generous expense account was a perk of being married, as if getting hitched was a business transaction rather than a lifelong commitment to love. I'd had sex for a living, and now that I was older and—I liked to think—wiser, there wasn't a credit card limit high enough to convince me to wed a man in exchange for material things.

"I'm not seeing anybody."

"But I just heard you say—"

"It's a long story."

I gave Debra a brief summary while I painted her nails in gradated shades of blue with white tips to remind her of her recent vacation in the Caribbean. Beaches to die for, she said, and some great boutiques if you knew where to look. At that point in time, I'd have settled for a two-week break in Guantanamo Bay if it got me out of going to the next round of Le Parade des Chefs with Jean-Luc and Marelaine.

But Debra was upbeat as always. "You like dogs, right? The puppy?"

"The imaginary puppy."

"There's a single guy in my yoga class who adores animals, and he's definitely got the right equipment, if you know what I mean."

"You're a married woman—should you be looking?"

"When he's wearing spandex, staring's practically unavoidable. Anyhow, I bet he'd be your plus one if I asked him nicely."

"Spandex?"

"Niles is insanely flexible, and the man's got stamina. You could do worse."

"Why's he single?"

"I overheard him telling Tiffany Meyers that his ex betrayed him, and he just couldn't forgive her for what she did. I guess she cheated, but that was, like, three months ago, so I doubt he's looking for a rebound fling. Do you want me to talk to him?"

What other options did I have? I might have exaggerated about my schedule for Marelaine's benefit, but I still had plenty of bookings for the next two weeks, so I didn't have time to start my own manhunt. And Debra seemed happy in her marriage, even if it wasn't the type of relationship I'd choose for myself. Could her suggestion really be that bad?

"Is that purse made from leather?" Niles asked after we'd introduced ourselves outside Nailed It. Debra had worked fast—a little over twenty-four hours after our conversation, and she'd already arranged a date with her flexible friend.

"Uh, no? It's Scotchgrain."

"That sounds like leather."

"It's PVC-coated canvas."

The Mulberry purse had been a surprise from Roxy last week, a late birthday gift she'd picked up on a trip to New York with Gideon. He had to travel for work, and he loved to take Roxy shopping when she tagged along. She said there were only so many trinkets she could use, so she'd started buying things for other people instead.

"Huh," Niles said, stepping back to peer at my feet. This evening, I'd worn a pair of fancy jewelled flip-flops with skinny jeans and a shimmery top. "Did you know that there's only a finite amount of plastic in the world?"

"Yes."

"Do you recycle?"

"As much as I can."

"Good. That's good. Well, shall we head to dinner?"

He walked off before I could agree, and I had to concede that Debra had been right about his physique. He'd worn a pair of perfectly-fitted slacks, and that butt... It was just a shame he seemed a bit...odd.

"Where are we going to eat?"

"Marie's Garden."

"That new fish place?"

He turned, aghast, his beautiful blue eyes widening as his chiselled jaw dropped.

"That's *Marine* Garden, and they murder tuna. And octopi, and plaice, and squid, and grouper, not to mention all the other innocent sea creatures that get caught up in the fishermen's nets. The health of the oceans is declining, and if we keep eating fish, even tilapia will be on the endangered list."

"I thought they farmed tilapia?"

"A travesty. Imagine spending your whole life in a watery prison, being fed on genetically-modified corn instead of plants and algae. It's inhumane."

Shut up about the fish, Imogen. Best not to mention the delicious grilled sea bass I'd eaten at Marine Garden with Stef last month.

"So you're a vegetarian?"

"A vegan. Do you know how much suffering exists in the dairy and egg industries? All the male calves and chicks that get slaughtered because man has deemed that they're not useful?"

Uh, I hadn't ever really considered that. But one thing I did know for sure was that almost every dish Jean-Luc created contained either eggs, cream, or butter—usually all three—and I was ninety-nine percent certain that his masterpiece at Le Parade des Chefs part deux would horrify Niles. No way could I take him as my date, even if I managed to overlook the other flaws that were becoming rapidly apparent. But nor could I make an excuse and hightail it home, because Debra had set me up with him, and she was a client who I couldn't risk upsetting.

I took a deep breath and kept walking, following Niles as he strode towards a shiny green Mercedes parked at the kerb. A *very* nice car. Sporty. Expensive. What did Niles do for a living? He didn't strike me as a businessman, but he obviously had money if he could afford a vehicle like that.

"This is your car?"

The Mercedes pulled away, and Niles gave its receding taillights a dirty glare. "Are you kidding? Do you realise how much fossil fuel that thing consumes?"

"Uh, no?"

I feared a lecture on carbon emissions, but Niles broke into a beaming grin instead. Boy, he looked really pretty when he smiled. The world was full of injustices.

"This is my vehicle."

I followed his gaze to the spot revealed behind the Mercedes, to...to... "What *is* it?"

"A rickshaw." He sounded like a proud papa. "Countries in the Far East have managed to develop an environmentally friendly mode of transport, and it's about time we brought that technology to the United States."

Technology? It was half a bicycle with a bench on wheels attached to the back of it, painted green and decorated with leaves and flowers. A sky-blue roof was folded down behind the seat.

"And you're the man to bring it?"

"Absolutely. I started Richmond Rickshaws last year, and now I employ seventeen pedalists. I've just taken on a new business partner, and we'll be branching out into Raleigh by the end of the year."

"Today Richmond, tomorrow the world."

He didn't pick up on the sarcasm. "Just the continental United States to start with, then maybe Europe. There's too much competition in Asia and South America."

"You'll be busy."

"Franchising, that's the best business model." He flashed me another devastating smile. "It's important to make time for my future wife and child too."

Well, he wasn't shy about his plans, was he? "Just the one child?"

"The planet's already overpopulated." He waved an arm at the bench seat. "Please, jump on board."

Any hopes I had of keeping my head down and staying incognito as Niles pedalled furiously towards Marie's Garden were quickly dashed when lights lit up around the edge of the hood and reggae music blared from speakers screwed to the bottom of the armrests.

"The electrics are powered by kinetic energy," Niles shouted over the noise of the cars blasting their horns as he got in their way. "Totally renewable."

Wonderful—at least my moment of mortification was eco-friendly. I arranged my hair so it covered most of my face as Niles bumped the rickshaw up onto the sidewalk to get around a traffic jam and nearly took out a pedestrian. Weren't there rules that these things had to follow? I hadn't even decided whether I wanted to be buried or cremated. Should I draft my last will and testament in a text message and send it to Stef?

Ten minutes later, Niles swerved in front of a pickup without signalling and pulled into the parking lot of Marie's Garden, oblivious as the driver cursed him out of the window. I'd survived. And if I couldn't get a cab back, I'd walk before I climbed on board that death trap again.

A neon sign above the door proclaimed Marie's was *100% Vegan, 100% Raw*. Dammit, I'd have to stop at McDonald's on my way home too. What on earth would I say to Debra when she asked me how it went?

"Here we are," Niles said, helping me down from his contraption. "Marie serves the best food in Richmond, and while we eat, you can tell me all about this problem Debra mentioned. Something about needing a man to attend a function with you because you're worried about going alone?"

"Oh, er, that... It got cancelled. Like, I got a phone call half an hour ago." My knees almost buckled when my feet touched the ground—a delayed reaction to several near-brushes with death. I hazarded a guess that rickshaw drivers didn't have a long life expectancy. Niles grabbed my hand to pull me upright, then dropped it just as quickly.

"My apologies, I should've asked before I touched you. Every woman has the right to bodily autonomy." True, they did, but no girl was gonna complain if a guy saved her from landing on her ass. "The event was cancelled? That's a shame, but at least we can enjoy dinner tonight."

Niles scooted on ahead to open the door for me, and I had to admit that in some ways, he wasn't so bad. During our dinner of seven-colour salad followed by frozen mango cake, which was surprisingly tasty, he lectured me on the destruction of the rainforests but also remembered to check my food was okay and ask if I wanted anything more to drink—non-alcoholic, of course. And he wasn't afraid to show his emotions— when he told me how he'd caught his so-called vegan ex eating the bacon sandwich that ended their relationship, he actually shed a tear.

Probably if I'd been an environmental warrior, hell-bent on saving the planet one pleather shoe at a time, he'd have been a good catch. But for me? Absolutely no way. Rickshaws or no rickshaws, there weren't enough nopes in the world, even if by the end of the evening, he'd made some good points about diet and left me considering composting. Although I did feel almost guilty for telling him I lived just around the corner and loved walking, then hiding behind a tree and begging Roxy to pick me up. Stef had a car too, courtesy of Oliver, but driving made her nervous, so she hadn't gotten the licence to go with it yet.

"How was the date?" Roxy asked when I climbed into her Audi, which thankfully had seat belts, airbags, and an excellent safety rating. Never again would I take such things for granted.

"Back to the drawing board."

"I think Stef might have a plan."

"Really?"

"She said she'd call you with the details tomorrow. The perfect man's out there somewhere, whether it's Jean-Luc or somebody else."

"What if I never find him?"

"You will. Fate's got a way of pushing people together. Look at Gideon and me."

"I thought it was Emmy who pushed you together?"

Emmy Black was one of the head honchos at Blackwood. Rumour said her methods could sometimes be a little unorthodox. From what I heard, she was so convinced that Roxy and Gideon were soulmates, she'd literally abducted him in an effort to make them date. Matchmaking taken to the extreme, but it had a happy ending.

"That too. But we're going to be more conventional this time. Regular dates with regular guys, absolutely no illegal activities involved at all. Don't worry; we'll find you a man."

    I only wished I shared her confidence.

CHAPTER 3 - IMOGEN

ME: WE HAD an interesting dinner, but Niles isn't quite my type. Thanks for introducing us though!

Send.

I'd just finished replying to Debra's *So how did it go?* text when my phone vibrated in my hand. Stef was calling.

"How did your date go?"

"On a scale of one to totally horrific, I'd rate it as terrible."

"Aw, really?"

"The high point was dessert, and the low point was almost dying in a rickshaw." I told her the whole story, including Niles's disgust when the girl at the table next to us asked for a bendy straw in her drink. "I'm beginning to rethink this whole stupid plan."

"Don't give up. We've only just gotten started."

"We? I'm wasting my time and yours, and shouldn't you be busy packing for your vacation?" In a week and a half, Stef, Oliver, and Abigail were jetting off to a fancy resort in the Caribbean. I tried not to be jealous, really I did, but I'd never been on a proper vacation in my life, and the thought of being stuck in Richmond while she sunned herself on a beach left me more depressed than ever. "Why can't I find a nice, normal guy?"

"The packing's going fine. Bridget's doing most of it." Bridget was their housekeeper. "And you might be in luck. I met an attorney yesterday, and since he's new in town, I volunteered your services to show him around. You know, the Capitol Building, Maymont, the Museum of Fine Arts, the botanical gardens... Inviting him to Le Parade des Chefs would seem perfectly natural."

"Did you mention it to him?"

"I figured it'd be better if you dropped it into the conversation after you met. That way, he'll already be besotted with you, and he'll agree to anything."

"Besotted. Right."

"Imogen, stop talking yourself down. You're a catch for any guy."

"So why do I always end up dating weirdos?"

"Because you need to aim higher." A pause. "And as I've said before, you should consider expanding your horizons beyond Jean-Luc. I know how much you like him, and eating his macarons is almost as good as sex, but he's...he's..."

"He's what?"

"He just always looks out for himself. Sure, he's polite and generous, but you're never going to come first."

"Thanks for your input, but I'm quite happy coming second."

"I didn't mean in bed."

"I know what you meant, okay? But Jean-Luc's everything I want."

Stef sighed. "So what shall I say to Matthew?"

"Is he an attorney from Oliver's firm?"

"No, from Ryman and Winkler. They're on the

other side of town. I had to deliver some papers for Oliver yesterday, and I got talking to Matthew in the lobby. He just moved here from Seattle two days ago."

"And he's definitely single? I don't want to upset his girlfriend if he's got one."

While Stef had gotten lucky with Oliver, I'd met enough attorneys in my former profession to make checking their marital status a priority. All those little hints that gave it away—a dent or a tan line on their third finger, phone calls that ended with a slick excuse, or a desire to avoid being seen in certain parts of town were massive red flags. One guy even had me bring a laptop on our "dates" as a cover story.

"He broke up with his last girlfriend when she got a new job overseas."

"And you think he's worth a try?"

"He didn't come across as the type to freak out if Jean-Luc serves up fois gras."

A definite check in the "plus" column.

"Okay, then let's do it. He can't be any worse than Niles."

Matthew really did have a Mercedes, a sporty three-door in midnight blue. The first thing I checked was his shoes. Definitely leather, and polished too.

"Imogen?"

"That's me."

He'd offered to pick me up from work to save me from walking home, and after the experience with Niles, I figured it was a good idea to get a look at his vehicle straight-off rather than risking another near-death experience. If he'd turned up with anything less than four wheels, I'd have pretended to be somebody else then texted my apologies, a trick I'd learned while working at Rubies.

Don't get distracted by his ass, Imogen.

Although it wasn't bad—not quite as toned as Niles, but now that I knew where Niles got his butt muscles from, I was more than happy to trade down. Matthew had made the effort to wear a shirt and tie, slicked back his hair, and shaved recently as well. Not a hint of a five o'clock shadow on that sharp jaw.

He bent to kiss me on the cheek, holding my upper arms gently. "It's nice to finally meet you."

We'd been texting back and forth in between his meetings and my clients. Since it was Thursday, which meant the Virginia Museum of Fine Arts was open until nine p.m., we'd decided to go there for a couple of hours followed by dinner at Ristorante il Mare, an Italian place that specialised in fish and seafood, but which also had several decidedly non-vegan desserts on the menu. I may have had a teeny ulterior motive when I selected where to eat—if Matthew enjoyed tonight's meal, he'd cope with anything Jean-Luc and his team might serve up.

"How was your last client?" Matthew asked. "I didn't think you'd be out so fast."

"Just straightforward infills, so they didn't take long. Better to be early than late."

"True. What are infills?"

"When a girl has gel nails and they grow out, there's a gap left behind. Every couple of weeks, the gaps need filling in."

"What happens if the whole gel thing falls off?"

"They're strong, so that rarely happens. How was your day?"

"I'm still learning my way around, but I took my first deposition this afternoon. That's when a witness makes a statement under oath but outside of court."

I already knew about depositions from hanging out with Oliver, but I nodded anyway as Matthew opened the passenger door for me. So far, this was a vast improvement on Tuesday's experience with Niles, but if the good vibes continued, how could I broach the subject of Jean-Luc's competition? I decided to wait until dinner. No point in scaring Matthew off right away.

"Have you always liked going to galleries?" he asked as I showed him around the exhibition of early 20th century European art. "You seem very knowledgeable."

"Ever since I was a little girl and I got my first set of crayons. I studied art history at the University of Richmond, but it's a hard field to find a job in unless you want to curate a museum or a gallery. I love looking at other people's work, but I like to create too. And I'm pretty good at talking to people." Or so my schoolteachers always said right before they gave me yet another detention. "That's why owning a nail salon is my perfect job."

"You own it? I thought you just worked there."

"No, I own it."

"That's a long-term commitment."

"Yes, but as long as business stays good, it'll pay dividends later on."

"What happens when you want a family?"

Well, that was hardly likely to happen anytime soon, was it? I couldn't even keep a boyfriend for longer than a month.

"I'll cross that bridge when I come to it. Hey, here's Duchamp-Villon's *Maggy*. A beautiful piece, but I'll admit I prefer his *Le Cheval*."

"It's not very well-proportioned."

Duh, it was art. The sculptor's vision. His magic. "That's part of its beauty."

"Hmm."

What did "Hmm" mean? The Picasso collection was met with indifference, although Matthew liked the Fabergé exhibition so he wasn't a complete heathen. I struggled to work him out. On the surface, he was perfectly civil, but there was also a touch of arrogance lurking beneath his smooth facade.

At the restaurant, the waiter showed us to a quiet table in one corner, screened by potted palms that muffled the chatter from the other patrons. A group in the middle—there for Laura's fortieth, judging by the personalised balloons—sang as a flaming birthday cake came out, the chocolate frosting sagging under the weight of the candles. Normally, I'd have joined in with the singing, but Matthew just gave the group a bemused look as he took a seat opposite me.

So he wasn't a party animal. That was okay. I'd dated plenty of good-time guys in the past because, with my background, I thought that was all I deserved. But seeing Stef and Roxy so happy, both of whom shared my chequered past, had encouraged me to set my sights higher.

I wanted a man who'd stick around for more than a few weeks, who'd love me for my flaws not in spite of them. Yes, I'd once slept with men for money, and I couldn't turn the clock back to erase my mistakes.

The question of when to tell a man what I'd done was always a difficult one. If I dropped it into conversation at the beginning, they either ran a mile or assumed I was a slut. If I left it too late, I risked the dreaded "Why didn't you tell me?" conversation, and they left anyway. Or worse, said they were okay with it when they clearly weren't.

A little over a year ago, I'd started seeing a guy who actually gave me hope. I'd confessed everything, and he still treated me like a human being. Then one night in bed, a night when I'd given him two orgasms and elicited a confession that it was the best sex he'd ever had, he'd rolled off, grinned, and asked how much he owed me. Of course, he'd laughed like it was all a big joke, but I still felt as though I'd taken a knife to the chest. Was that how my love life was destined to be? Always plagued by reminders of a time I'd rather forget?

Perhaps that was one reason I liked Jean-Luc so much. I'd been to his apartment plenty of times, and one evening over too much wine, I'd told him about my time with Rubies, about my many regrets and my hopes for the future. He'd just given me a hug and said, "The past is the past. It's tomorrow you need to focus on."

But he'd shown no signs of wanting to be involved in that tomorrow as anything more than a friend. *Yet*. I had to stay positive.

Matthew brought me back to the present with a question. "Red or white?"

Decisions, decisions. I liked both, and I could never pick. If I were out with the girls, I'd go for rosé, but I didn't think Matthew would appreciate pink wine. White went well with seafood, but a softer red like

Pinot Noir was also acceptable. Did I mention I'd once dated a sommelier?

"Whatever you're having," I finally said. There, that was easier.

"A bottle of Chablis, then."

That turned out to be the easiest question of the night. I'd barely taken a bite of my shrimp salad when Matthew decided to delve into the only thing I hated discussing more than my career history.

"Tell me about your family, Imogen."

Oh, hell no. Even Jean-Luc didn't know about them. "I'd rather not."

"You don't get on? Come on, you must have some good memories. What about your father?"

"My father's dead."

To me, at any rate. Saying he was six feet under sure beat admitting he was serving life for armed robbery. My brother should've been locked up too, except he'd skipped bail ten years ago when I was seventeen, and I hadn't seen him since. And my mother? I'd never forgive her for not protecting me from them.

"I'm sorry to hear that. And your mother?"

I pushed my food around my plate, my appetite having deserted me. "Who knows?"

"You don't know whether she's dead or alive?"

"Would you mind if we talked about something else?"

Matthew shrugged and popped a dough ball into his mouth. "Of course. Earlier, we briefly touched on your employment status. What are your future plans for the salon? Sale? Expansion? Or do you just want to paint nails for the rest of your life?"

He managed to make the job I enjoyed so much sound like a bad thing. "I'll probably paint nails."

"But if you moved into a management role and opened more salons, you'd make more money."

"Money isn't everything."

His quiet snort said he didn't agree, and the date only went downhill from there. What were my grades like at school? Had I made retirement plans yet? How did I feel about public versus private education? Since I never wanted to see him again, I just made stuff up as his questions got more and more ridiculous.

Why didn't I walk out? Because I'd already ordered dessert, and nothing got between me and Ristorante il Mare's espresso Martini tiramisu. That stuff was heaven on a plate, even worth putting up with an arrogant ass for twenty more minutes.

"So, Imogen. What's your favourite dish to cook for a boyfriend?" Matthew asked as the waiter set my dessert on the table in front of me. "You do cook, don't you?"

"Of course I cook." As long as microwaving counted. "Have you ever tried honey-roasted pig trotters? My great grandma passed the recipe down through the generations—it's kind of a family secret, but I bet you've never had anything like it. All the jelly oozes out, and I swear it tastes better than it smells. How's your panna cotta?"

"It's okay." Matthew crinkled his nose and put his spoon down. "I'm surprised you have time to make such an unusual dish. How do you fit everything in? Do you have a cleaner?"

Sure, because I was made of money. "No, I have a robot."

"A...robot? Like a Roomba?"

"Yes, but I also have one on legs that dusts. My cousin's a robotics engineer in Japan, and he sent me a prototype to test out. Once he upgrades the software, it'll wash the windows too."

"Impressive. I'd like to see that. And I suppose you could learn to cook a wider variety of dishes." He nodded to himself, seemingly weighing up my suitability as his future mate. "How many men have you kissed?"

I choked on a mouthful of tiramisu as he looked on, impassive. That utter prick. This was basically a job interview for a position I didn't want. Still, I managed to conjure up a sickly smile as I forked in my last mouthful of dessert.

"Are we talking just this month?"

"What? No, I meant ever."

"Oh, I have no idea. I gave up counting after the first fifty. None of them ticked all my boxes, you know?"

He pushed his plate away and motioned to the waitress. "Check, please! Imogen, how do you want to split this? Straight down the middle?"

Nice try. He'd eaten the lobster while I ordered pumpkin ravioli. "Perfect. Since we've already established I'm not so good at math..." I giggled. "Why don't you work the amounts out while I use the bathroom?"

Fortunately, I'd been to Ristorante il Mare enough times to know there was a fire exit right next to the ladies' room, and it was never locked. I made good use of it. Matthew and his inner misogynist could take care of the check while I went home and rued my terrible luck with members of the opposite sex.

Chapter 4 - Imogen

"I'M SO, SO sorry," Stef said. "Matthew seemed perfectly normal when I spoke to him."

I cradled the phone in the crook of my neck as I poured myself a glass of wine. After putting up with the aforementioned idiot all evening, I deserved one. The only alcohol I had in the apartment was half a bottle of flat champagne leftover from Stefanie's visit last week, which reminded me once again that I needed to go shopping.

"Men like that are good at hiding their true characters."

A made-to-measure suit, a sixty-dollar haircut, a holier than thou attitude...at least in public. I'd met dozens of Matthews in my former job. Those assholes wanted the recognition and respect of their peers, and having the right woman on their arm was just another part of the act. And by the right woman, I meant a wife who'd pander to their every need and turn a blind eye when they cheated with girls like me.

"I should've asked Oliver's opinion. He's better at picking out sleazes. He's still at the office, but when he comes back..."

"I'm not sure I want to try the blind date thing again. Perhaps I should just try the old-fashioned way and look for a guy in a bar?"

"That's not always safe. What if someone spikes your drink?"

"I'll drink out of the bottle and keep it with me."

"I'm still not sure that's the best way. Too many single men in bars are only after one thing, and that thing isn't a trip to a cooking contest."

"Perhaps I could do an exchange?"

I kicked off my pumps as I walked through to the living room, and they landed under the coffee table next to yesterday's shoes. When I got stressed, I didn't have the energy to tidy up.

"That's basically selling yourself again. If you're going to go down the transactional route, why don't you just call Octavia and ask if she knows any male escorts?"

"That's... That's...actually not a bad idea." Octavia was our old boss from Rubies. Of course, Rubies had gotten closed down after the police investigation Stefanie got caught up in, but Octavia had already opened up a new agency. Although she only booked women, she had plenty of connections in the industry, and I bet that included men too. The only problem? Escorts like us didn't come cheap, and I couldn't go bargain basement if the guy was gonna meet Jean-Luc. Most of my money was currently tied up in Nailed It, which meant maxing out my credit card was the only option. "Perhaps I could try the bar idea first, and if that doesn't work out, I'll call Octavia next week."

Stef tried again. "I'm not sure you're going to meet Mr. Right in a bar."

"Hot guys have to hang out somewhere. They don't stay at home alone on Friday nights."

"Then how about I come along and be your wingwoman? Or Roxy? Or both of us? I can't do tomorrow because Oliver's out and I have to take care of Abby, but I'm free on Saturday evening."

"I guess I can wait until Saturday."

"We should go to The Brotherhood of Thieves—you know, the place with the motorcycle in the middle of the bar?"

"Isn't that a bit rough?"

"Not anymore. It's more hipsters than bikers now. City boys with pristine leather pants and Harleys they ride twice a year. Oliver took me there last week, and the French fries are to die for. Really crispy."

Dammit, she knew French fries were my weakness. Better even than chocolate. But after my last two dates, an evening at a hipster hangout-slash-biker bar could hardly be any worse, could it?

"Sure, let's go there. Why not?"

"That's the spirit. I'll organise a car and pick you up at eight."

With a plan of action in place, I could spend Friday evening relaxing at home instead of heading out on safari to Richmond's classier nightspots. And when I said relaxing, I meant trying on potential outfits for the trip to Le Parade des Chefs and realising none of the zippers did up anymore. Those damn French fries. I wasn't much overweight, and men liked curves—I knew that for a fact—but I didn't have the time or the money to buy new clothes before next week.

So, correction—Friday night would be spent in the gym instead of on the sofa. At least spandex stretched.

If I got up early every morning between tomorrow and next Sunday and spent half an hour doing cardio before I went to Nailed It, *and* lived on smoothies, I'd fit into my favourite dress again. I may not have been able to do much about my height, but that little blue number matched my eyes as well as giving me better cleavage than Marelaine. The sacrifice would be worth it.

Wow... They'd redecorated the whole gym since I last visited three months ago. Okay, eight months ago. January third, to be precise, when my rock-solid New Year's resolution crumbled at the first mention of cocktails. Back then, the walls had been blue and grey, kind of drab, but now they'd changed to in-your-face purple and mint green. Most of the machines were new too, which would have been a good thing if I'd known how to work any of them. Why wouldn't the stupid treadmill go faster than a walking pace?

"Do you need help?" the guy next to me asked as he jogged along.

"Uh, how do you make it speed up?"

"Press the red button to cycle through the modes, then the arrows to increase and decrease."

I wasn't sure what was more impressive—his taut muscles or the fact that he could have a conversation while running without gasping for breath. I followed his instructions, then grabbed the handrail to keep my balance when I got sidetracked by his ass.

"Are you okay?"

"I'm good. Just tripped."

This was why I didn't go to the gym more often—it was dangerous. The year before last, I'd ended up twisting an ankle, which meant I couldn't wear pumps for six weeks.

"You should clip on the safety cut-out strap. That way, the belt'll stop if you fall off."

He reached over and passed it to me. Yes, I was the only person using the safety strap, because everybody else managed to run in a straight line.

"Thanks."

"No problem. Shall I give you a hand with connecting your headphones to the TV?"

"I didn't even realise that was possible."

Before I could blink, he'd reached over, tapped away at my console, and then I was back in the eighties with cheesy electropop blaring in my ears. I quickly turned down the volume before I got deafened.

"Okay?" my new friend asked.

I nodded.

"I haven't seen you in here before."

"It's been a little while since I've come."

At least, a little while since I'd come without using either my fingers or a vibrator. Could my luck finally be changing? Had gym karma blessed me with a solution to my man-related problem? This guy was polite and helpful, his ring finger was bare, and since he was working out on a Friday night, I had a faint hope he was between girlfriends too.

"I spend too much time here. The endorphin rush gets addictive, you know?"

Not as addictive as chocolate chip cookies, but I agreed anyway. "I'm not sure I can run long enough for the endorphins to start."

"Just build up slowly. Better to do that than pull a muscle. Do you want me to give you a rundown on how the machines work?"

"Would you mind?"

"Give me ten minutes to finish my program, and I'll show you around. I'm Drew, by the way."

"Imogen."

He held out a hand, and I nearly fell off the treadmill again as I reached out to shake it. Luckily, he held me upright as he grinned.

"Good to meet you. Hopefully, we'll see a lot more of each other."

Chapter 5 - Imogen

"EASY, TIGER."

DREW steadied me with an arm around my waist as I stumbled against a chair and almost fell over again. This was starting to turn into an alarming habit around him, although since we were now in a bar rather than the gym, that sort of behaviour was marginally more acceptable.

Earlier, he'd patiently helped me to work the elliptical trainer, then given me tips on my form while I struggled with the weight machines. I realised at that point I'd been missing a trick—if this was the kind of man who hung out in the gym, I should have started going there months ago. All that time I'd wasted in bars and clubs...

After I'd taken a much-needed shower, I found Drew sitting in the reception area, his blond hair damp and curling over his collar.

"Are you waiting for somebody?" I asked.

"Yes. I mean, uh, hopefully. You." He stumbled over his words. Cute. "I was wondering if you'd be interested in going out for dinner?"

"Tonight?"

"No time like the present. Unless you're busy, and then we could arrange another day. Any time you want. Unless I'm working late, but I usually finish by seven."

Drew was a manager at a software company in town. Not a programmer or anything geeky like that—sales and marketing was his thing. He'd started off working at the head office in Maryland before transferring to Richmond last year to set up a new branch. A promotion he couldn't turn down, he said, although it was tough starting again.

Didn't I know it—when I quit Ohio and moved to Virginia, I'd felt utterly alone in the world. A psychologist would probably have told me that was why I took the job with Rubies—because, just for a night at a time, I felt wanted. But now I'd set my sights higher, and much of that was due to Stef's belief in me. I owed her a lot.

And for me, dating a sales manager sure seemed like a step up. I mean, at least he had a steady job, and one that was legal.

"I'm free tonight, but I'm not exactly dressed for dinner."

"You look beautiful."

Really? My cheeks heated, not just because of his words, but because of the sincerity behind them. I was wearing the first thing I'd grabbed out of the closet, a navy-blue jersey dress, a wrap-around that tied at the side. I'd bought that style in four different colours because it was so comfortable.

"In that case, let's go. Do we need a cab?"

"My car's parked on the street."

Another Mercedes, but dark red this time. Tasteful grey leather. And when he started the engine, soft classical music played from the speakers. I feared he might head for somewhere pretentious, but instead, he drove us to a cheerful Mexican joint where we made a mess with tacos and drank too many margaritas. Or at least, *I* drank too many margaritas. Drew had one and then switched to water.

When the pitcher was empty, we headed to the bar next door and danced until the early hours. I hadn't enjoyed myself like that with a man for months, not since I accidentally went out with a slimeball who turned out to be engaged with a pregnant fiancée at home. Drew swore he was single. I'd asked him at least three times on the dance floor.

And now he hung on to me as I tried, and failed, to find the exit. One in the morning, and the bar was about to close.

"You're not going to be sick, are you?" he asked.

"No, I'm fine. Good. Really good, actually." I might have giggled.

"Do you want me to fetch the car? Or can you walk?"

"Uh…" I was supposed to be walking, wasn't I? That was what gym addicts did. "I'll do the feet."

Two blocks felt like a marathon as I hung onto Drew, but I made it back to the Mercedes, and Drew strapped me in with my purse in my lap. This time, the quiet strains of Tchaikovsky helped me drift off to sleep.

"Hey, where are we?"

"Nearly home."

"But I don't live here."

My apartment was in the city, but trees lined both sides of the road we were on, dark due to a lack of streetlights. My heart pounded as I tried to work out what was happening. *Thump. Thump. Thump.* How long had I been out?

"I thought we'd go to my place." He reached over and laid a hand on my thigh. High. Too high. His fingers inched upwards towards my panties. "You said you were okay."

I slapped his hand away. "Yes, I am, but not for that. We've only known each other for a few hours."

The third date. I wouldn't sleep with a man until the third date. That was the self-imposed rule I'd set six months ago. Sick of being used, I'd sworn that never again would I sell myself out the way I did at Rubies, that I'd get to know a man properly before I went to bed with him.

"We like each other, don't we?"

"Yes, but..."

Did I like Drew? I'd thought so, but now I wasn't so sure. Little beads of sweat popped out on the back of my neck as I realised he might not be everything I'd assumed.

"Then what's the problem?"

"Just take me home."

"Sure, I'll drop you back in the morning."

"No, now!"

I made a grab for the wheel, but Drew gripped my wrist and twisted.

"Let go! You're hurting me."

"Are you crazy? We could've crashed!"

"Take me home!"

Gravel crunched under the tyres as Drew hit the brakes and pulled to a halt at the edge of the road. Now what? My breath came in sharp pants while he took a long inhale.

"Imogen, what's wrong?"

"You've kidnapped me."

"We're on a date. You had a good time at the Mexican place, didn't you? Don't you think you're getting a bit hysterical?"

Was I? I *had* enjoyed myself in the restaurant.

"I guess."

"And then you fell asleep. I didn't want to wake you to get your address. That's hardly kidnapping. Now, can we carry on without you trying to kill us both?"

I really wasn't sure what I wanted to do, and my head was so, so fuzzy. Maybe I should just go with him? That would be the easiest option, right?

"Okay."

He flashed a grin at me, his teeth gleaming in the moonlight. "Good girl."

Then his hand moved back to my leg, and he leaned across the central console. The moment his lips met mine, I wanted to vomit. How could I have been so wrong about him?

"Get the hell off me!"

"You want this. You know you do."

"No, I don't."

"You've been giving me signals the whole evening. Your hands were all over me in the bar."

"Only because...because..." We were dancing. Where else was I supposed to put them?

"Just relax, all right? You were practically asking for me to fuck you."

This time, he put his hands on my cheeks as he forced his tongue into my mouth, and his fingernails dug in as I tried to push him away. Shit, shit, shit! Even at Rubies, I'd never gotten into a situation like this one, mostly because I always stayed sober when I was with a client. Alert. Took precautions like letting Octavia know where I was and meeting in a hotel or a restaurant, never a dude's freaking car.

Drew let out a yell as I bit his tongue and loosened his grip as I jerked away.

"What's your problem?"

"What's *my* problem? I said no!"

He shook his head faintly. "Crazy bitch. I sure do pick 'em."

"And you're a sick freak!"

"Shut up!"

He followed his words with a slap hard enough to let me see stars. Combined with all the alcohol I'd drunk, the blow made everything fade to black for a second, and as my eyes flickered open again, Drew started the engine.

I scrabbled for the door handle, and pain shot through one of my fingertips as a nail tore off. But I got the door open and the seat belt off then landed on my ass on the hard-packed dirt outside.

And what did Drew do? He laughed. He fucking laughed.

"Where're you gonna go, Imogen? You're in the middle of nowhere."

"Just get the hell away from me."

He reached over and yanked the door shut, and I choked on exhaust fumes as he roared off down the road. The only saving grace was that my purse had fallen out of the car with me, and I slowly flipped onto my hands and knees to feel around for the spilled contents. Where was my phone? I needed my phone.

"Stef?"

"Imogen? Is that you? It's almost two o'clock in the morning."

"I did something really, really stupid."

"What? Where are you?"

Good question. The night air and the jolt to my spine had helped to sober me up, but I still didn't have a clue.

"Sitting beside a road somewhere. I don't know."

"Can you use the GPS on your phone?"

"I... I..." A tear plopped onto the screen as I swallowed down a sniffle. "It's all blurry."

"What on earth happened? Are you okay?"

"I accidentally met another asshole. He left me here." Now the tears came thick and fast. "I don't... I can't..."

Oliver's voice came through the phone, muffled. "Tell her not to move. I'll call Blackwood."

That was it. Enough was enough.

Tomorrow, I'd join a convent.

CHAPTER 6 - IMOGEN

TWENTY MINUTES LATER, a car slowed as it approached. I'd retreated into the protective embrace of the overhanging trees to stay out of sight, because at that moment, I trusted nobody but my friends and whoever Oliver was sending to help me. Could this be my rescuer?

My phone buzzed in my hand—a text from a new number.

Unknown: Imogen, Sofia should be arriving any second. She's driving a silver Prius. Sloane (Blackwood).

I sagged in relief when I realised they'd sent a woman to pick me up. And better still, she wasn't driving a Mercedes. I'd never get in one of those again. They were a bad omen. I stepped forward to the edge of the asphalt, and sure enough, a silver car stopped alongside. The headlights illuminated the rest of the contents of my purse, and a twinge of pain shot through my back as I stooped to collect the scattered items.

"Let me do that."

A dark-haired woman crouched alongside, picked up my pepper spray, and shook the canister.

"You didn't use this?"

I'd forgotten I even had it. "No."

"Keep it in the outside pocket of your purse, that way it's always at hand. I'm Sofia, in case nobody told you."

"Sloane mentioned it."

"She's organised like that. I hear you had man trouble?"

"I was stupid."

"Takes two to tango, honey. You didn't end up standing beside a deserted highway on your own."

"He said it was my fault. That I'd led him on."

"Tell me what happened."

She helped me into the car, and only once we'd started moving did my trembles subside. Tell her what happened? Somehow, it was easier to talk to a stranger about the nightmare of the last week, this dark-haired, silent stranger who listened intently and nodded in the right places, never belittling me or judging. As Sofia drove, I spilled out all the horrible, messy, awkward details about Jean-Luc and Marelaine and Niles and Matthew and Drew, the remaining dregs of alcohol loosening my tongue, and I found a strange catharsis in sharing. I'd never gotten on with therapy, but perhaps it'd be a worthwhile investment after all? Goodness knows, I had enough demons to exorcise.

I was still talking when Sofia pulled up outside my apartment. I hadn't given her my address, but it didn't surprise me that she knew it.

"Will you be okay here alone? I can take you to Stef's if you prefer. It's only a few blocks farther on."

"I don't want to disturb her, not with the baby, and my roommate'll be home." My new, slightly odd roommate, Svetlana, who only ate green food and stood on her head in the living room for ten minutes every morning to get her day off to a balanced start. "And, uh, thanks for listening. I'm sorry to burden you with all that."

Sofia patted my hand, and her fingers were oddly hot to the touch.

"Sometimes, it's good to talk. And don't worry—I'll fix it."

She'd what? "No, no, you don't need to do anything. I'm off men for good. Unless a miracle happens and Jean-Luc asks me out, I'm staying single."

And unfit. First thing tomorrow morning, I'd cancel my gym membership and spend the money I saved on movies and candy. If this week was any indication, being a couch potato was a far healthier lifestyle. Perhaps I could even save up for a new sofa?

"Honey, some men need to be taught a lesson, and Drew's one of them. Jean-Luc needs educating too." She climbed out and glided around to my side of the car. "I'll walk you inside."

"There's no need—"

"Yes, there *is* a need. Get some sleep, and I'll call you in the morning."

"He did *what*?" Stef screeched. She still had a key, so she'd turned up in my bedroom at seven a.m. with coffee from Java and an expectant look on her face. "Your text said you were home and everything was fine. That is *not* fine."

"I survived, okay? And look on the bright side—we don't need to go barhopping this evening. How about we watch a movie instead?"

"Back up. Back up. *Rewind*. Drew can't get away with what he did."

"Now you sound like Sofia."

"Sofia? That's who came to collect you?" Stef perched on the edge of my bed and began twiddling the ends of her hair, a nervous habit of hers. "This just gets worse and worse."

"What's wrong with Sofia? She seemed nice."

"Sofia's a madwoman."

"Are we talking about the same person?"

"My height, dark brown hair, ski-jump nose, kind of pushy?"

"I guess that description fits. Who is she?"

"One of Emmy's close friends. How much did you tell her?"

"Uh, everything? She said she'd fix it."

"Freaking hell. Drew's a dead man."

Right now, I didn't see how that was a bad thing. "Don't you think you're exaggerating a teeny bit?"

"No, he really is. Sofia was the one who kidnapped Gideon."

"I thought that was Emmy?"

"She helped, but apparently it was Sofia's idea."

"Well, whatever she has planned, Drew deserves it. He abandoned me next to a damn forest. I could have gotten eaten by a bear."

"We only have black bears near Richmond, and they're mostly scared of people."

"Okay, a wolf. Or a cougar. Or I could've died of hypothermia."

"It's summer."

"Are you defending him now?"

"Of course not. I'm just saying that I know Sofia

better than you, and moderation isn't a word that's in her vocabulary."

"Good. I stand by my earlier comment." My ass had a massive bruise, my head throbbed, and when I took a sip of my coffee, pain shot through my jaw where Drew had hit me. "Let her do her worst."

Oh, if only I'd known what her worst would be. But at that moment, I was still living in blissful ignorance, so when my phone vibrated on the nightstand, I picked it up.

"Hello?"

"Right, everything's arranged," Sofia said. No preamble. Not even a greeting. "I've found a guy to go to that cooking contest with you, but in return, you have to go to a thing with him tomorrow. He needs a plus-one. Bradley's coming over with outfits at seven a.m. You know Bradley, right? Emmy's assistant?"

Huh? My brain frantically tried to process her words, and all I could do was channel Stef. "Back up a second. What thing? What guy?"

"It's a wedding, but his ex is gonna be there and they don't get along so well anymore. He needs to prove he's moved on."

"Have you lost your mind?" Now I understood exactly what Stef meant. "I can't go to a stranger's wedding with a guy I've never met before."

"Oh, but you have met him. Apparently, he prevented you from being arrested when you accidentally dated a drug dealer last year."

"I'm not a hundred percent sure he was a drug dealer. He was just friends with a drug dealer." Because that made all the difference when the cops were on their way to search the apartment I'd been sleeping in.

Hazy memories of that night trickled back. Of a brown-haired hottie sent by Blackwood hammering on the door and driving me home in the middle of the night. "Wait. Do you mean Malachi?"

"So you *do* remember him? Good. Yes."

At the time, I'd asked for his phone number, although I probably wouldn't have been brave enough to call it. Malachi was way out of my league. Word came back from Oliver that he had a girlfriend, and I hadn't thought about him since. Unless you counted the dirty dreams. I might have had a few of those.

"I can't date Malachi."

"You're not *dating* him. Think of it as more of a business arrangement. He'll be in Third Base tonight from seven."

"Third Base?"

"It's a bar downtown. You can meet him there to hash out the details."

"But—"

"You want Jean-Luc, don't you?"

"Yes, but—"

"Well, Malachi's the perfect guy to help you get him. He's trained for undercover work, and he'll keep his hands firmly off. How are you feeling, by the way?"

"A little better. What's happening with Drew?"

"Don't worry about Drew. Seven o'clock. Third Base."

She hung up, and I stared at the phone open-mouthed. What just happened?

"Was that Sofia?" Stef asked.

"How did you guess?"

"With that look on your face, it had to be either Sofia or Emmy. Nobody else inspires such bewildered frustration. What did she want?"

I gave Stef a brief précis of the conversation. At that moment, I longed to crawl back under the quilt, squash the pillow over my head, and sleep until Le Parade Des Chefs was over. My stupid pursuit of Jean-Luc had brought me nothing but trouble.

"Are you gonna go this evening?"

"Are you as crazy as Sofia? How can you even ask that question?"

"I hate to admit it, but she does have a point. She's offered you the perfect sidekick for making Jean-Luc jealous. I know I'm engaged to Oliver, but I'm not blind, and Malachi's ridiculously handsome. And safe."

"Do you know much about him?"

"No, but nobody working for Blackwood would pull a stunt like Drew did last night."

From everything I'd heard, Stef was right about that. And when Malachi rescued me before, he'd been the perfect gentleman and walked me right upstairs to my apartment before disappearing back to the Batcave or wherever it was that he came from. And—I wasn't sure whether this was a plus or a minus—since he'd been on the team for the Carter case, which was what we'd all been wrapped up in at the time, he had to know my history. At least I wouldn't need to pretend with him.

"What about this wedding?"

"Weddings are fun. Just go along, smile a bit, and eat cake."

"You really think it's a good idea?"

"I think it's a better idea than trawling Richmond's bars in search of a willing victim for our original plan. At least if it's a fair trade with Malachi, you won't feel guilty about using him to hook Jean-Luc."

"Why do I feel like I just made a deal with the devil?"

"Oliver always says that on the streets of hell, there are angels in disguise."

Chapter 7 - Imogen

WELL, I GUESS I knew where I fell in Malachi's list of priorities. Instead of taking the time to meet me somewhere civilised to discuss tomorrow's awkward arrangements, he'd made me venture far outside my comfort zone, all the way to Third Base on the edge of downtown. Why did he like this place? The name alone should have been enough to put any sane person off. And it looked awful from the outside, all peeling paint and dirty brick with an ancient neon sign that buzzed as it flickered.

"Shall I come inside with you?" Stef asked. "Oliver doesn't mind waiting."

"I'll be fine."

She gave me a dubious look.

"Honestly. There're plenty of people around."

"What time shall we pick you up?"

"I'll get a cab home. There's no need for you to come out late." And they'd already gone out of their way to help me.

"But—"

"Get Malachi to bring you back home," Oliver said. "You shouldn't be walking around alone in this area."

"What if he's been drinking? Or he doesn't want to?"

"Ask him to ride in a cab with you. He'll do it if he

doesn't want to get his ass kicked by Emmy on Monday morning."

Third Base stank of stale beer and second-hand cigarette smoke. All heads turned as I walked in, and the only other women in the place were the redhead behind the bar who looked twice my age and tough as old boots, and a skinny girl playing pool at the back. Her opponent rested his beer gut on the table as he stared at me too.

Where was Malachi? I didn't want to make eye contact with any of these people, so I tiptoed around a puddle of something sticky and headed for the bar instead. Sports played on a TV next to the register, and I had to raise my voice to be heard above the commentator.

"I'm supposed to meet a guy called Malachi," I told the redhead. "Do you know who that is?"

She extended one skinny finger past my left shoulder. "Over there, sweetheart."

I turned and let my eyes adjust to the gloom. The table she'd pointed at had two occupants, their seats angled so they could see the screen. Furthest away in a gloomy corner was a young black man in his early twenties. A stranger. His companion watched me carefully, and even across the room, I felt his penetrating gaze.

Malachi.

I started towards him, my feet dragging all of their own accord. He waited until I reached the table before he stood up.

"Hey."

"Hi."

This wasn't awkward in the slightest.

"You have this seat, and I'll get another one. Wasn't sure whether you'd turn up or not." He jerked a thumb towards his companion. "This is Deon."

I perched on the edge of the wooden seat, one of many that littered the room, and pasted on the fake smile I'd perfected during my time with Rubies.

"Hi, I'm Imogen."

"Yeah, Mal said you were coming."

"Are you watching the..." I glanced across at the TV. "Uh, the baseball game?"

Up close, Deon looked younger than I'd first thought, maybe seventeen. Should he even be in a bar?

"Lady, everyone here's watching the baseball game. That's the whole reason you come to Third Base."

I squinted at the screen. The Washington Nationals were beating the Chicago White Sox with three innings left, according to the caption at the bottom. I wasn't about to admit I didn't know what an inning was.

"Who are you rooting for? The Nationals?"

He pointed at his White Sox jersey, and I awarded myself zero out of ten for observation.

"Oh. Of course. Do you play yourself?"

This time, he pointed lower, and I groaned out loud when I realised he was in a wheelchair. Dammit. Couldn't I manage to say one thing, just *one* thing, without putting my foot in it?

"I'm so, so sorry."

"Forget about it."

"I should have noticed."

"I'd rather people didn't."

Thankfully, Malachi came back to save me from myself. Earlier, I'd dreaded the prospect of being alone with him, but now I wished I was.

"What do you want to drink?" he asked as he dumped a battered chair beside mine. "They don't serve cocktails here."

"Just water." No way was I getting drunk again, not after last night's experience. In fact, total sobriety looked like an excellent option. "Do they have sparkling?"

"Who knows? I'm not sure anyone's ever ordered water in here before."

Deon snorted out a laugh, and I wanted to sink into the floor. *Eyes on the prize, Imogen.* Survive the next week, and I might get Jean-Luc. Then I'd never have to meet another man for dinner or drinks ever again.

Malachi headed to the bar, leaving me alone with Deon again. Somehow, this managed to be more awkward than my "dates" as a Ruby, and considering I'd once been to dinner with a man who forbade me to make eye contact and insisted on talking about himself in the third person at all times, that was a big statement to make.

"Do you come here often?"

When all else failed, resort to what sounded like a terrible pickup line.

"Whenever Mal has time to bring me. Once a month, something like that."

"You're friends?"

"Why the fuck d'you sound so surprised about that?"

"I'm not. I mean, I guess... Isn't he quite a lot older than you?"

"We're neighbours, okay?"

"I'm sorry. Again."

The grease-stained menu took on a new fascination

as I waited for Malachi to come back, although I felt too sick to contemplate eating anything. Half of the words were obscured by questionable splodges anyway.

"Hungry?" he asked, setting a glass of water down in front of me. Still, no ice, no lemon. And the glass was chipped. "They didn't have sparkling."

Was it too late to change my mind about Matthew? Even acting like a Stepford Wife was preferable to this, and I'd only have to keep up the pretence until the cooking contest was over.

"I'll eat when I get home. Could we just quickly go over the plan for tomorrow? Then I can leave you to watch the game in peace."

Malachi raised an eyebrow to Deon, who shrugged. They were speaking a strange form of sign language I didn't understand. Was this something they learned in high school while the girls were having the talk about periods?

"She's not Erin," Malachi said.

"She looks like Erin."

"What? She looks nothing like Erin. This is a favour for a friend. That's it."

Deon glowered at me. "Bitches are all the same."

I tried for another smile even as tears pricked at my eyes. "Perhaps it's best if we just call this off. There's obviously been some sort of misunderstanding."

I got halfway out of my seat before Malachi shook his head and fixed me with those piercing blue eyes. Against his brown hair and a day or two's worth of stubble, the effect was striking, and it reminded me why I'd never quite forgotten him. But I'd changed in the time since we first met. With every day that passed, I felt more tired, and it became harder and harder to keep projecting the fun persona I'd adopted as a shield.

Nobody liked a misery-guts, that's what my mom always used to tell me. Too bad she'd contributed to that misery, first by turning a blind eye to the abuse I'd suffered, and then with her continued support of a husband serving life in the Stateville Correctional Center and a son who should have been alongside his father.

When I left Ohio, I'd vowed to put the dark times behind me, but life still had a way of wearing me down around the edges, even when I'd come so far.

"No, we're good. My ex..."—Malachi grimaced —"said some shitty things to Deon, and I didn't find out until recently. Neither of us wants that to happen again."

"It won't. I want this week to be over as much as I'm sure you do."

"Sofia said you needed a date for a fancy dinner to make some guy jealous?" Malachi ran a hand through his scruffy locks. "Apparently, I need to dress smart and get a haircut."

"I just don't think he sees me as girlfriend material at the moment."

"And you want to show him otherwise?"

"Yes, and that way if he splits up with the horrible Brazilian girl he's seeing, he might give me a second glance."

Malachi snorted. "Any asshole that doesn't give you a second glance is either blind or gay. Guess I'd better dig out a suit."

"Don't you need the suit for the wedding we're supposed to be going to tomorrow?"

"Uh, no? Sofia didn't tell you?"

"Tell me what?"

"Fuck." Malachi raised his eyes to the ceiling. "My buddy's marrying a porn star he met playing an online video game, and they're having a beach wedding."

My brain didn't even know where to start with that. I was still stuck on "porn star" when my jaw hit the damn table.

Malachi just looked resigned. "Yeah, that was pretty much the reaction of all of us who know him too."

"But... But... Richmond doesn't even have a proper beach."

Only the occasional strip of sand along the James River, but I couldn't imagine why anyone would want to get married there. If the weather was good, every spot would be crammed with picnicking families, teenagers drinking beer they shouldn't have, and dogs shaking dirty water over unsuspecting passers-by.

"The beach is in Fort Lauderdale."

"Florida?"

"The wedding doesn't start until three. We fly out at ten."

"And when do we fly back? I have work on Monday morning. My first appointment's at eleven."

"We can leave right after dinner if you want. I have to be in the office for a meeting at ten."

"Why exactly do you want me there? Sofia said you needed to prove you moved on?"

"Because Erin's a psycho," Deon put in, and Malachi's jaw clenched.

"That's not helping, bud."

"Is it true?" I asked.

Before either of them could answer, a waitress slid two plates of food onto the table—giant burgers dripping with cheese, sizzling onion rings, and a mountain of fries. Malachi's came with a side of pickled jalapeños, and he popped one into his mouth before stacking a pile inside his burger. My mouth burned just watching him.

"How can you eat those things?"

"I've always liked spicy food."

"He ate a habanero once," Deon said. "A whole one, seeds and everything."

"The moral of that story is never make a bet with Emmy. You know Emmy?"

"I've met her. Isn't eating habaneros dangerous?"

"I spent the next fifteen minutes in the bathroom, alternately blowing my nose and scrubbing my tongue with soap."

"Soap?"

"It doesn't taste so bad once you've scalded off your taste buds." He pushed his plate an inch towards me. "Want a French fry?"

Had somebody told him that they were my kryptonite?

"Maybe just one." Or two. Or three... "We were talking about the wedding?"

"Yeah, we were." His sigh hinted at the unspoken word at the end of the sentence: *unfortunately*. "I can't skip it. Archie's always been there for me, and I also want to find out whether this woman's likely to take him for everything he's got."

"You haven't met his fiancée?"

"*He* only met her six weeks ago."

"Holy shit."

"Exactly."

"And your ex is going? Is that Erin?"

"She's friends with Archie's sister. They're both bridesmaids. She keeps telling everyone I want her back and won't leave her alone when it's the other way around, and it's getting embarrassing."

"Do you think she'll be nasty to me?"

Silence from Malachi, but Deon spoke up.

"She's a two-faced bitch. Watch your back."

On the plus side, it seemed Deon didn't hate me quite so much now. But did I really want to jet off to Florida to be a target for a crazy woman? Staying single for the rest of my life seemed like a more appealing option with every passing moment.

But I'd made a deal, and now acquaintances of Stef and Roxy's were involved in my problems too. If I backed out, I wouldn't just be letting down Malachi, I'd be letting down my friends.

I was tough. I could do this. After escaping the horrors of Cleveland and surviving my time as a Ruby, a few hours at a wedding should be a walk in the park.

"Where do I need to meet you tomorrow?"

"I'll pick you up at nine."

Chapter 8 - Imogen

"I'M COMING, I'M coming."

Five past seven, and Bradley was already trying to hammer my door down. It had been almost midnight when Malachi and Deon dropped me home in Malachi's truck, and I'd even go so far as to say I enjoyed myself at Third Base. Once Deon realised I wasn't a permanent fixture in Malachi's life, he'd taught me the basic rules of baseball, and the White Sox had turned it around and won. I'd celebrated with my own plate of perfectly crispy French fries while Malachi bought a round of drinks for everyone. Due to the debacle with Drew, I'd stuck with lemonade, and Malachi had Coke because he was driving. Only Deon drank beer, and nobody seemed to care he was underage. I'd kept my mouth shut too, not wanting to ruin the truce he seemed to have called.

"Hurry up," Bradley shouted. "These bags are heavy."

Only because he'd brought half a department store with him. Shoes, purses, make-up, and...twenty different bikinis?

"Didn't you get the message? We're going to a wedding."

"Yes, on a beach. I love your nails, by the way."

I'd fixed the broken one and repainted them in

fuchsia. Marelaine's words got to me, okay?

"But I still need to wear a dress or something."

"Nuh-uh. The dress code is 'strictly swimwear,' and I didn't think you'd be a one-piece girl. They're doing photos of everyone in the sea afterwards, so I haven't brought anything white just in case it goes see-through. Plus people might think you were the bride."

"Swimwear?" That had to be a joke, right? "Who has guests wear swimwear to a wedding?"

"The future Mrs. Archie Curtis. The invite's in one of the bags if you want to check. Didn't Malachi tell you?"

"No, he conveniently forgot to mention that part."

"You might be able to wear a sarong for the reception. I've brought a selection. Plus some floaty tops, sunglasses, and a whole rainbow of flip-flops. And sunblock! You must remember to wear sunblock. Your skin's so pale—you'll burn otherwise. Now, sit down so I can sort out your hair."

"A bikini?"

"Think positive, doll. If you're not wearing a cover-up, then Malachi has to go shirtless, and that man is *fine*."

Okay, so that was a small plus point, but he still should've warned me. That way, I could have gotten a spray tan at least. And avoided eating those fries last night. Never again would I make a deal without full disclosure of the facts first, no matter how desperate I was.

"A bikini?"

Malachi closed the truck door, put my bag in the back seat, and climbed into the driver's side before he answered. Today, he'd worn a pair of shorts and a tight white T-shirt that proved Bradley wasn't lying about his chest, which went some way to mollifying me. Yes, I was aware of how shallow that sounded, but there had to be a few perks to this stupid arrangement.

"Are you mad at me?" he asked.

"Yes."

He glanced across, sheepish. "Sorry. I didn't think you'd come if I told you in advance. But I figured wearing a bathing suit wouldn't be a problem for a girl like you."

He...*what*? Oh, no, no, no. Tell me he did *not* just go there. A girl like me? Just because I used to be an escort, he thought I'd be happy to parade around half-naked? That... That... I didn't even bother to finish the thought before I tumbled out of the truck and slammed the door so hard the glass rattled. He could take his "strictly swimwear" and shove it up his ass.

I fumbled in my purse for my keys as I ran back into the building. Forget the elevator—I took the stairs two at a time, heart pounding as Malachi's footsteps sounded behind me.

"Imogen?"

"Get lost!"

I didn't breathe again until I'd locked my front door behind me, and then I sucked in ragged gasps of air because the sprint up the stairs had highlighted my total lack of fitness. Would I ever escape from my past? Bad enough that I still looked for my brother in every dark shadow without being bulldozed by my reputation when I least expected it.

My hands were shaking. Actually shaking. Anger and frustration bubbled to the surface, and I thumped the dining table as my first tears leaked out. One brick at a time, the walls I'd carefully built around myself were crumbling, and I didn't know how to shore them up.

Soft knocking made me jump.

"Imogen? I'm sorry. I didn't mean that the way it came out."

"Leave me alone."

"Will you let me explain?"

I didn't bother to answer, just hurried into my bedroom and closed the door behind me. Thank goodness my roommate had gone to visit a friend this weekend instead of being around to witness the drama. Was it too early for wine? Oh, I almost forgot—I'd drunk it all.

On another day, I might have gone to the store, but with Malachi outside, I regressed to my childhood and burrowed under the quilt instead. Not that it had ever helped. When I used to hide from my brother that way, he still found me every single time.

Then I heard a strange scratching noise, and my bedroom door opened. What the hell?

"Did you just break into my apartment?"

Of course he did. I knew damn well I'd locked the front door.

"I was worried about you."

"I'm fine. Do me a favour and go away."

"You're not fine. You're crying." Malachi sat on the edge of my bed, and I couldn't muster up the strength to wipe my tears, let alone push him away. "Imogen, I'm sorry. I realise how what I said sounded, but all I meant was that you're beautiful."

Huh?

"Believe me, I'm the least likely person to take a jab at somebody over their past because I know exactly how that feels."

"What's that supposed to mean?"

"You're not the only one with a time in your life you'd rather forget."

"I bet you didn't end up selling yourself to make ends meet."

"I might have if I hadn't been such a Neanderthal." He paused. "Maybe then I wouldn't have ended up in prison."

Prison? *Prison?* The word sent a chill through me, an icy rush that froze my blood and turned my thoughts sluggish. My father was in prison, and if there were any justice in the world, my brother would have been his cellmate.

That Malachi had been inside put him on their level, and the thought of being so close to a criminal left me nauseous. I tightened the quilt around myself instinctively, and the hurt in his eyes said my reaction didn't go unnoticed.

"W-w-what for?" *Dammit, Imogen. Keep your big mouth shut.* "S-s-sorry. I mean, that's none of my business. Forget I asked."

He shrugged, a nonchalant gesture when the tension in his frame said he was anything but relaxed. The fingers of his left hand picked at a loose thread on his shorts before he shoved his hands into his pockets.

"I used to steal from the rich to feed the poor."

"Like Robin Hood?"

He gave me a lopsided smile. "I was the poor."

"Oh."

"I figured the folks I took money from had plenty of it, and some of them were real assholes. That was my downfall."

"Why? What happened?" Even though I knew I should keep my mouth shut, I couldn't help asking.

"I broke into the wrong house."

"It had an alarm?"

"Yeah, but I bypassed that. Even back then, I was good with electronics."

And locks, it seemed. I thought back to how quickly he'd got into my apartment and shuddered. Once he'd gone, I'd drag the sideboard across the door at night until I could convince the landlord to fit a bolt on the inside.

"I can still see the place now," Malachi continued. "A huge mansion over in Rybridge, his 'n' hers Porsches in the driveway, swimming pool, chandeliers and original paintings in every room. But the couple came home while I was in there."

Holy crap. That was worse than the time I got caught by a client's wife. She chased me through the house with a golf club until her husband tackled her in the living room.

"And they caught you in the act?"

"No, I hid. Figured I'd wait until they went to sleep then leave. But they got into a fight in the hallway, and I honestly thought the fucker was gonna kill his wife, so I stepped in and stopped him."

Wow. That wasn't the ending I'd expected.

"But that makes you a hero."

"The judge didn't see it that way. The husband ran out and called the cops, and they arrived while I was waiting for the ambulance."

"Didn't they give you leniency or something? Seeing as you saved a woman's life?"

"Turned out the husband was an attorney, and they threw the book at me."

"But he beat up his wife."

"Those assholes stick together. Half of them are crooked or worse. I got two years, and he got a smack on the wrist until he killed her six months later and got put away for manslaughter. Three years." Malachi gave a hollow laugh. "*Manslaughter*. He murdered her, and his sentence was only one year longer than mine."

"So he's out now?"

"Nah, he only lasted three months inside. Picked a fight with the wrong guy. Nobody in the Deerfield Correctional Center likes arrogant attorneys."

While I could never condone cold-blooded murder, it did seem as if the man got what he deserved. Poetic justice served up prison-style. Malachi had managed to stay out of trouble, and if his current job was anything to go by, he'd used the experience to turn his life around. I loosened my grip on the quilt a little, because even though he was an ex-con and he'd walked into my home uninvited, I didn't feel threatened.

"Were you in the same prison as him?"

He shook his head. "I got sent to Indian Creek."

"What happened when you were released? You got a legitimate job?"

That was what I'd done after I quit the escort business. I began working as a barista, and even though the money was worse, I found living with myself much easier. The biggest rewards weren't always monetary. When I glanced around my bedroom, I was weirdly proud of what I'd achieved against the odds.

But Malachi just snorted in a manner that reminded me of Deon. "Any idea how many people are willing to employ an ex-con? Not many."

"So what did you do?"

"While I was inside, I took a horticulture course. Don't laugh—it was all part of my grand plan to start a cannabis farm. At the time, I thought it was a smart idea, that it'd be safer than burglarising places, but when the time came to walk out of the prison gates, I swore I'd do everything I could to avoid going back there. Am I boring you yet?"

"No, but if you don't want to talk about it..."

"Figure I owe you an explanation for behaving like an asshole earlier." There was that wonky smile again, and my heart gave a skip.

"I might have overreacted a tiny bit. I guess that my past's such a big part of me that sometimes I jump to conclusions, and I'm sorry."

"Nothing to apologise for."

A tear rolled down my cheek, not because I was upset, but because he was being nice to me. My emotions were all over the place this week.

"Here." He passed me a tissue. "Want me to go?"

Strangely, I didn't. "How did you go from horticulture to security work? Isn't that a big jump?"

"Yeah, it is. For months, I couldn't get any job at all. I went to fifty-seven interviews, but nobody wanted to employ a scruffy homeless guy who'd barely scraped through high school."

"High school was my refuge. I spent as much time there as I could so I didn't have to go home."

Why did I just tell him that? I hardly told anybody

about my childhood, and especially not people I'd only just met. Stef knew the basics, and I'd made a drunken confession to Octavia one night many years ago, but that was it for people in Richmond. Even Roxy didn't have a clue. I'd been glossing over the details for so long now that it'd become second nature, at least until I was confronted with a man who let me see into his damn soul. I bit my lip so hard it drew blood, and Malachi must have understood my pain because he gave me a small smile but didn't push the matter.

"I didn't go home much either. Too busy hustling."

"So how did you end up working for Blackwood?"

"Did you know Emmy and her husband run a charity foundation?"

I shook my head. They were notoriously secretive, and I'd only heard snippets about them from Stef and Oliver, and occasionally Roxy.

"They support the homeless in Richmond, and the pastor at the soup kitchen referred me to their project for help. A week later, I was working as a gardener at their estate. They gave me somewhere to live, a wage, and most importantly, their trust. I owe them everything, and all they've ever asked is that I pay it forward."

Something clicked in my head. "Is that why you take Deon to watch baseball?"

"He's a good kid, but his mom works three jobs, and he's stuck at home a lot of the time. If he makes his grades at school, we go out and do shit." Malachi finally stood up. "But enough about me. Do you need anything before I head off? More tissues? Ice cream? It's probably too early for wine."

"You're leaving?"

"I still have to fly to Florida. But don't worry—I'll go alone. It was wrong of Sofia to push you into this in the first place."

So many revelations in such a short time, and my brain was still struggling to sort through them. Malachi wasn't who I thought he was, that was for sure. Since I met him last year, I'd elevated him to some mythical Superman figure in my mind, a hero who swooped in to save girls from their own stupidity. Finding out he wasn't all that different from me was...unexpected. Yes, the shadier parts of his past had surprised me—perhaps even alarmed me, if I was honest—but if I couldn't see past those to the person he'd become, then I'd be guilty of double-standards.

"Wait!"

He stopped halfway to my bedroom door, turned, and raised one gorgeous eyebrow.

"I'll come with you." I tried to get out of bed, but my legs got tangled in the quilt, and I tumbled to the floor. "Owww!"

"Fuck." Malachi was at my side in an instant to hoist me up by my armpits. "Are you hurt?"

"I just landed on my bruised ass."

Now we were standing close. Too close. I took a pace back because sharing Malachi's airspace made my breath hitch.

"How the hell did you bruise your ass?" he asked.

"Sofia didn't tell you?"

I was starting to see a theme here.

"Sofia provides information on a need-to-know basis only, and she obviously thought I didn't need to know."

"Well, the night before last, a ride home went really,

really wrong..." I gave Malachi a brief summary of my week so far—three disastrous dates and a rescue by Sofia in the middle of the night. "And that's why I can never go back to the gym."

His mouth set into a hard line. "Sofia's handling it?"

"That's what she said."

"Good. It means I don't have to. Your bag's in the other room, Imogen. There's no way you're coming to Florida. This wedding's gonna be a total fuck-up, and you've been through enough already this week."

"I'm fine. The bikini Bradley picked out covers almost all of the bruise."

"That wasn't what I meant."

"I know, but we have a deal."

"Look, I'll still come to this thing with you next Sunday if that's what you're worried about."

"You will?"

"It's my duty to keep you safe, and it seems the best way to do that right now is to help you find a guy who isn't going to take you out for dinner and then assault you afterwards."

And Malachi needed to avoid girls who were psychos, as Deon put it. "In that case, it's *my* duty to help out with your Erin problem."

"Erin's a bitch, and I'm not putting you in the line of fire."

"I'm good at ducking. And my emotions may have been a mess this morning, but underneath, I'm a survivor. She won't break me." I put my hands on my hips. "I'm coming to Florida, even if I have to take a cab to the airport and fly commercial."

To my surprise, Malachi smiled, and my heart sped up.

"And there she is."

"Who?"

"The fiery girl I met last year."

"You remember me from last year?"

"You're not a girl who's easy to forget." The smile turned into a grin as he held out a hand. "Let's go to the damn beach."

Chapter 9 - Imogen

THE REDHEAD LOOKED me up and down, and her lips curled into an unmistakable sneer.

"Imogen." Erin repeated my name as though it was a dirty word. "Are you one of Misty's colleagues?"

She meant Misty Nights, AKA the porn star, and it was fairly obvious I wasn't since I'd just walked in with Malachi. But Erin needed to get her digs in. He'd warned me she would.

"Oh, no I'm not." I forced a giggle. "I guess it's easy for you to get confused since we're all in bikinis. Yours is from Target, right? I saw it on one of those giant billboards along the interstate."

She narrowed her eyes. "It's Tommy Hilfiger."

"Oops, my mistake." Score one to me.

My own bikini came from Jessika Allen, a make I'd never heard of but which lifted my girls to perfection. When I walked out of the tiny bathroom on the plane where I'd contorted myself into beachwear, that was the first place Malachi's gaze had strayed. Thankfully, his friend Cruz, a colleague from Blackwood's Florida office, had given us a ride to the beach house where the wedding was being held, avoiding the need for a cab. I'd covered up with a filmy sarong for the trip, twisted and tied at the back of my neck, but once we arrived, I stripped it off for Erin's benefit.

Strangely, I felt more confident now. For so long, I'd used my body as a tool, and it was easy to fall back into old ways. This wasn't the first party I'd attended with a virtual stranger, my only job to look pretty—and I wasn't stupid, I knew I was pretty—and act out the role I'd been hired to play.

I looped my arm through Malachi's and smiled sweetly at his ex as she gathered herself together for another shot.

"I guess you'll be looking for the buffet table," she said. "It's right over there by the pool cabana."

Malachi was absolutely right—Erin was a first-class bitch. I leaned in close.

"Ooh, lovely. Is there cake? I'd hate to lose my curves when Malachi's so fond of them."

This time, she turned her scrawny behind on me and marched off in her pumps. Who wore heels to a beach party? A gaggle of girls on the far side of the terrace welcomed her with a cocktail, and when a couple of them glanced across at me, I knew she was telling them all about Malachi's horrible new companion.

"Nice job," Malachi said, grinning. "Can I get you a glass of wine? I think we both need one after that."

"I'm avoiding alcohol at the moment. After what happened on Friday, I might never drink again."

"I promise I'll get you home safely. Sofia would kill me if I let anything bad happen, Erin's barbs aside."

"Honestly, I'd rather keep my wits about me today. What time is the ceremony?"

Malachi glanced at his watch. He might have dressed like a beach bum, but he wore a Breitling. Working at Blackwood obviously paid well. But before he could answer, a blond guy sidled up to us.

"Forty-five minutes," he said.

"Nervous? Having second thoughts?" Malachi asked. "There's still time to back out." Ah, this must be the groom. "Archie, this is Imogen. Imogen, meet Archie Curtis, soon to be Mr. Misty Nights."

A momentary hint of panic flashed in Archie's eyes, but then he mustered up a smile. "No second thoughts —Misty's the one. And you're Malachi's...date? Girlfriend? Or did he just meet you at the airport and win you over with his charming personality?"

"Date," I said, at the exact same time as Malachi blurted out, "Girlfriend."

Archie laughed as he patted Malachi on the back. "Smooth, buddy. Real smooth." He leaned in closer. "Is Erin behaving herself?"

"Imogen'll keep her in line."

"Just watch your back and hers. Last night, I overheard Erin telling my sister that bridesmaids always get lucky, and it's no secret she wants you back." Archie glanced over at me. "Sorry."

"It's okay; she knows."

Yup, I was just the hired help.

"I didn't invite her to be a bridesmaid, I swear. But Livvy said she'd help with the organising, and before I knew it, she'd bought outfits for them both. Livvy's my sister," he explained for my benefit.

"It's okay, I understand," I told him. "Just forget Erin and enjoy your wedding. It's a huge step, and you shouldn't have to worry about trivialities. Do you need to go and get changed?"

He glanced down at his white swim shorts. "No, I'm wearing this. We did consider adding a bow tie and cuffs, but Misty said I looked like a stripper, so we decided against it. Bad optics, especially with Misty having announced her retirement from acting."

"She's quitting porn?" Malachi asked.

"Not entirely. She's still going to direct." Archie shrugged. "Being a lead actress, she's had too much unwanted attention lately, plus she's committed to making this marriage work. And so am I. I know everyone thinks I've lost my mind, but I really love her. She's sweet, she's kind, and she'd rather eat pizza and play video games than go out to parties."

"Bet she whips your ass at the games."

Archie blushed. "I don't even care. Say, while you're here, can I ask your professional opinion on something?"

"Sure."

"Archie," someone yelled from across the garden. "Can you check we've put all these chairs where they're supposed to be?"

That flash of panic came back. "I'd better go. Talk later."

"Good luck," Malachi said. "See you on the other side."

Archie dashed off, leaving us alone for a moment on the uppermost patio. Despite the informality of the dress code and the slight chaos around us that could only have been caused by leaving everything to the last minute, the happy couple had chosen a striking venue for their upcoming nuptials. The gardens of the huge beachfront mansion reached right to the edge of the sand in three wide terraces, each edged with tropical plants in full bloom that filled the air with a delicate aroma. The swimming pool next to the house had a waterfall at one end, and half a dozen people had already claimed sun loungers while they sipped their cocktails.

High walls at the boundaries meant the whole property was private apart from the area by the sea, and security guards loitered on the beach, checking for trespassers. Another pair had checked our invitation when we arrived, sweating in their uniforms as they manned the gates. I thought that was quite impressive, but Malachi had rolled his eyes and muttered something about rent-a-cops. Clearly, there was a hierarchy in the secretive world of security.

"This sure is a big house," I said to Malachi. "Someone must've worked really hard to afford it."

"They did, quite literally. Apparently, it belongs to a friend of Misty. They film adult movies here. Let's hope the pool has a good filtration system, huh?"

Oh. Perhaps my apartment wasn't so bad, after all.

"I'm not such a great swimmer anyway. Have you seen Misty?"

"Only on screen."

"Excuse me?"

Malachi closed his eyes. "Shit, I did it again, didn't I? I meant, Archie and Misty sent video invites to the wedding as well as the paper ones. I absolutely have not watched my friend's future wife getting her kit off. Fuck, I need a beer."

He took my hand and led me towards the buffet table, which groaned under the weight of platters and bottles. Mostly bottles. Ice buckets held two different kinds of champagne, and a guy who looked like a fitness model stood at the ready with a cocktail shaker. Shirtless, of course. I took a moment to admire his six-pack, but it wasn't a patch on Malachi's.

"Can I offer you a drink, ma'am?"

"Something non-alcoholic, please."

"At this wedding? Are you sure?"

I noticed a half-empty glass of red next to him. How much of a circus was this going to be if even the bartender had resorted to drinking?

Malachi squeezed my hand. "I said I'd get you home."

"In that case, perhaps I'll just have a small glass of champagne." A little something to take the edge off. That could only help if I had to put up with Erin for the entire evening.

"Here you go? Are you related to Misty? Her sister?"

"No, I haven't even met her yet. Why?"

"You just look similar, that's all."

I suppose I'd received worse compliments. Liquid courage in hand, I joined Malachi in making small talk until it was time to head to the beach. In some ways, he reminded me of myself, like his ability to move smoothly from one inconsequential topic to another, never touching on anything controversial with people he didn't know. I'd quickly learned how to converse with strangers as a necessity in my former job, and I suspected he'd had to master the art for whatever undercover work he did with Blackwood.

Then it was time for Archie to sign his life away. A young brunette—Livvy, Malachi whispered—stood on a table and shouted for everyone to go down to the shore. Two blocks of seats had been set out on either side of a central aisle, and a bower of white roses provided a backdrop for the ceremony. Beautiful. And the best part? When Erin tried to walk across the sand in her four-inch heels, she freaking sank.

"She never did think things through," Malachi muttered.

After two men had lifted her free, she opted to go barefoot instead, and Livvy kicked off her white flip-flops so they matched as they followed Misty and her dog down the aisle. Yes, her dog. She was being given away not by her father but by a cocker spaniel in a tuxedo. The dog was better-dressed than any of the other guests.

"Isn't Tico adorable?" the girl next to me whispered. "Misty said that until she met Archie, he was the only man in her life who'd been totally loyal."

Perhaps I really should get a dog? Loyalty sure sounded like an attractive option, and they probably didn't require as much maintenance as men. Just a walk every day, and bathroom breaks, and a couple of meals...

"Do you, Chastity Ann Roker-Haynes, take this man, Archibald Robert Curtis, to be your lawfully wedded husband?" the officiant asked.

Oh my gosh. Misty's real name was Chastity? Boy, that was ironic. But she looked so happy standing up front with Archie and her dog, both of whom were panting in the heat. She'd worn a cream bikini, jewelled at the edges, and a veil that fell all the way to the sand was pinned into her blonde hair. With her looks, she could have been a model, but I knew from experience that her height would work against her. At sixteen, I'd been told by every agency I was too short for the runway.

Then they were man and wife, and when the

officiant said Archie could kiss his bride, the only thing that broke them apart was the best man coughing like mad from behind. An unusual match, but they were clearly in love.

Would I ever have a day like this? I'd always fantasised about a fancy outdoor wedding with a ballgown of a dress, a bouquet of roses, chrysanthemums, and orchids, and a hundred friends watching me walk down the aisle alone to say "I do" to the man of my dreams.

Oh, who was I kidding? I could count my friends on my fingers, and as for the man...

"Before I came, I'd have put money on a divorce within six months," Malachi whispered. "But now I'm not so sure."

Okay, I might have dreamed about him last night, but that's all it was: a dream.

"Archie seemed happy earlier. Nervous, but happy. I hope they last."

"Me too. Not just because Misty-slash-Chastity seems okay, but because the last time he had a bad breakup, he insisted on a boys' trip to Vegas, and I woke up by the side of the road in the desert with no recollection as to how I got there. In a fuckin' dress."

Now, that I wished I'd seen. "What kind of a dress? Something slinky?"

"Does it matter?"

"Well, since we're supposed to be dressing up next Sunday, I'd like to understand your sense of style. I mean, was it neon and ruffles or something more tasteful?"

"It was pink with feathers, okay? Fuck knows where it came from. A showgirl at the casino, probably, since that's where we were drinking earlier. Which is why I go easy on the alcohol now. No man wants those sorts of pictures doing the rounds more than once in his life."

"They were on Facebook? I'd almost be tempted to join up just to see."

"Just email. I steer clear of social media because of work. You're not on Facebook either?"

No, because if I existed on the internet, it would give my brother a better chance of finding me. On my Rubies profile, I'd kept my face in shadow and, like all the girls, I'd used a false name. After ten years, I hoped he'd given up looking, but since I was the only thing standing between him and a jail cell, I couldn't afford to take that risk. I should have kept my mouth shut all those years ago. Mom knew where he was hiding, of that I was sure, which was why I'd told her I lived in Sacramento.

"I'm not sure it's safe. So many people pretend to be who they're not."

Around us, guests started to meander back towards the mansion. According to the printed cards that had been on each of our seats, we had two hours to "relax and chill" before we all posed for photos and sat down for dinner on the terrace. I was looking forward to the speeches, not because they promised to be entertaining but to get some pointers. Stef had asked me to be maid of honour at her upcoming wedding. A bittersweet honour, since it was yet another reminder that everyone but me had landed a perfect man. The date hadn't been set yet, but I couldn't see her waiting much longer now that baby Abigail had been born.

"What do you want to do?" Malachi asked. "Get more drinks? Food? Take a swim?"

"Could we just sit on the beach for a while? I can't remember the last time I walked on sand."

A tiny white lie—I'd only been to the beach once before, with a client who paid me to accompany him on a long weekend to Miami. The days had been okay, just sitting around while he golfed, but he'd pushed me into letting his friend join in the night before we left, and I'd never forget the constant grunting.

"Sure. Let's go find some towels."

To Misty's credit, she'd thought of everything, and the towels were sitting in a basket at the edge of the lawn. I unrolled mine next to Malachi, who apart from a bit of hand-holding for Erin's benefit had been the perfect gentleman. Unfortunately.

No, Imogen. Not unfortunately. I needed to keep my eyes on the prize, and the prize was Jean-Luc. Malachi was just a means to a hopefully happy ending.

"Do you come to Florida often?" I asked.

"Maybe a couple of dozen times since I started with Blackwood. But last year, I had to spend three weeks here on a case, so I got to know the guys in the Fort Lauderdale office. And the best beaches, and a few of the bars."

"Work hard, play hard, huh?"

"Something like that. Undercover work can be a bitch, but sometimes it has its perks."

"Do you think you'll keep doing security work for the rest of your life?"

"What else would I do? Go back to horticulture? Yeah, I'll stick with Blackwood. Working there's more than just a job; it's a calling. And those guys are family now."

That was exactly what Stef said. Once they accepted

you as one of their own, they always had your back. I'd felt a little stab of jealousy when she told me, and again now with Malachi because I still felt more lonely than I ever let on, especially since Stef spent most of her time with Oliver and Abigail at the moment.

But I smiled and nodded because that was what I always did. And I shouldn't have been complaining, because I'd gotten a free trip to the beach, I had a cute guy beside me, and Bradley had even remembered to pack sunblock so I wouldn't burn.

I held up the bottle. "Any chance you could do my back?"

"Sure. We get bonus points if Erin's watching."

Malachi had surprisingly soft hands, and he was thorough. Oh boy, was he thorough. I was halfway to heaven by the time he rocked back on his heels and placed the bottle by my outstretched hand.

"Your turn."

Two could play at that game. Octavia had encouraged all of her girls to take a massage course, and I'd passed with flying colours. When Malachi lay out on his front, I dug in with my thumbs, then spotted Erin staring at us from the second terrace. And she looked gloriously annoyed.

"Erin's watching us," I whispered.

"Good."

"And I don't like her very much, so I'm just going to..." I swung one leg over his ass so I was straddling him, one knee either side of his hips. "Do this. Okay?"

"Nice idea," Malachi mumbled.

I might even have gotten a moan out of him as I went to work, and so engrossed was I in the thick cords of muscle that ran either side of his spine, I didn't even notice when Erin disappeared. Oops.

"There, all done." I crawled back to my own towel, albeit somewhat reluctantly. "I'm gonna go and get a drink. Do you want anything?"

No answer.

"Malachi?"

Nothing.

Well, that was a first. My magic hands had sent a man to sleep.

Chapter 10 - Imogen

"ANOTHER GLASS OF champagne?" the bartender asked as I approached. "Or a cocktail? It's definitely a cocktail sort of a day."

Should I? I deserved it after surviving the ceremony. "A cocktail, but just a small one. And is there a bathroom nearby?"

"There's one in the pool house, but Mindy just headed over there. Probably best to try the mansion. If you go in through the terrace doors, cross the great room, then take the left-hand hallway through the double doors, there's a half-bath second on the right."

"Across the great room, left-hand hallway, second on the right," I repeated. Directions had never been my strong point.

"Should I draw you a map?" he asked good-naturedly.

"No, no, I'll be fine." I could always ask somebody if I got lost, couldn't I?

I walked past groups of people chatting on the top terrace, and from the snippets I heard, they fell into two camps—those discussing the state of the porn industry and those expressing concern that Archie had suffered some sort of breakdown.

Since I didn't know much about either, I just hurried on past through a room with no less than twelve sofas, four of them clustered around a sunken area lined with fur rugs, and skirted an abstract statue of a couple fucking. Part of me wondered why nobody had covered it up, seeing as Archie's parents seemed to be a rather conservative couple in their mid-fifties, but I was also weirdly impressed that Misty didn't try to hide who she was. I'd never have been brave enough to flaunt my work for Octavia, even if I'd wanted to.

Across the great room, take the right-hand hallway, second on the left...

Wait.

This wasn't a half-bath. It was a dining room. A dining room complete with Erin snorting a line of cocaine off a polished mahogany table that seated at least fourteen.

Shit, shit, shit.

Before I could back out, she straightened, wiping traces of white powder from under her nose.

"Well, look who it is. Malachi's piece of trash."

Oh, that little witch! Who was she calling trash? At least I'd worn an outfit that covered more than my nipples.

"Considering you dated him for months, I'd think about how that statement reflects on you."

"I know he's just trying to get back at me for that night in New York, but I was drunk when I slept with the guy, okay?" Her voice rose alarmingly, and she began waving her hands. "It doesn't count if you're drunk!"

She'd done the dirty on Malachi? What a piece of work. "It does count."

Now she squared up to me, hands on hips. "You're telling me you've never done anything stupid involving alcohol?"

"Sure I have. I've just never cheated on my boyfriend. No wonder he wants nothing more to do with you."

"Really? You think? Then why does he keep calling me?" She fumbled her phone out of her bikini top and waved it in my face. "Look—missed calls!"

The phone was moving too much for me to see properly, but I couldn't imagine Malachi stalking her, not after everything he'd said to me.

"He probably pocket dialled."

"And he probably hired you from an escort agency, dime store Barbie."

Despite all the shit I'd lived through, until that moment, I'd never slapped another woman. But my palm connected with Erin's cheek before I could stop myself. And with the scream she let out, you'd have thought I'd gouged out her eyes with a freaking spoon.

"Yeeeeeooouuuw!" She flew at me, crimson with anger, clawing at my face as she screamed obscenities. Aw, hell. My heart took off at a crazy gallop, and I tried to get away, but she wound one fist around my hair and hung on as she spat her insults.

"You fake-ass floozy! You're nothing but a cheap whore. Nothing!"

In desperation, I hooked one leg around hers and kicked the way my old self-defence instructor had taught me. She landed on her skinny behind with a bump, but she still didn't let go, so I ended up sitting on top of her.

"I'm gonna pull these stupid extensions out!" she yelled.

"They're not freaking extensions! Get the hell off

me!"

I pushed at her face with both hands, and she tried to bite my fingers like the rabid dog she was. I adjusted my grip, but so did she, using one hand to grab at my bikini top and pull. My boobs popped out, and she screeched even louder.

"Fake! Fake! Fake! Everything about you's fake!"

Running footsteps sounded from behind, followed by a sweet Southern drawl.

"What the actual heck?"

Fingers tipped with pearly white nails tried to pry Erin's hands out of my hair, but she'd gotten too good a grip. What did she do in her spare time? Jell-O wrestling?

"Benny! Mitchell! We need some help in here."

Two hefty guys tore Erin's hands away from me, and the taller of the pair lifted me up by my armpits as she scrambled to her feet. Even then, she wasn't finished, and Misty grabbed her arm when she ran at me again.

"Enough! What on earth's going on?"

Oh, shit. I tried to cover my boobs with what was left of my bikini top while I spluttered apologies. "I'm so, so sorry. I don't know what happened, but—"

"She hit me!" Erin shrieked.

"Is that true?"

"I know I shouldn't have, but she called me a dime store Barbie." And an escort, which had cut far too close to the bone.

"Erin, why can't you...?" Misty started, but then she looked past her, gaze focused on the table. "Are you taking drugs at my freaking *wedding*?"

"I... No, it was her."

Erin pointed at me, but since she still had flecks of white powder clinging to the skin above her lip, her lie wasn't all that convincing. And thankfully, Misty saw right through it.

"Get out, Erin. Just get out."

"But—"

"I don't want to hear it. Nobody takes drugs around me. *Nobody*."

"I'm here for Archie, not you."

"Do you want me to get him? Because he'll say exactly the same thing."

"Really? You think? You only met him six weeks ago, and I've been friends with his sister for a decade."

Misty's shoulders slumped, conciliatory, and for a moment, I mistook that for a lack of backbone. But Misty was an actress, albeit not a mainstream one.

"Perhaps you're right. I mean, six weeks since meeting someone in person for the first time isn't really long, is it? I guess all those phone conversations, the ones that kept us up every night for the last freaking *year*, they didn't count." She gave the tiniest jerk of her head, and the two men stepped forward. "Get rid of her."

As the two men picked Erin up—literally, one at the head, one at the feet while she writhed like a snake between them—I allowed myself the tiniest smile. But it didn't last for long because Misty turned to face me instead, and one of my stupid boobs popped out again.

"I'm so sorry," I said as I tried to tie the torn pieces of spandex together.

"Same." She sighed, perching on the table. "Archie always said Erin was volatile. Neither of us wanted her here, but his sister's had some problems recently, and he felt it was important for her to have her friend's support." Misty swept her hand over the table, puffing the remains of Erin's coke into the air, and for a moment, her face twisted in anger. "I hate drugs, and she knows that." A pause. "My brother died from an overdose."

I wished mine had. "I... I'm sorry for your loss."

My entire vocabulary around this lady consisted of apologies. I needed to get a thesaurus. And as the adrenaline began to wear off, emotions got the better of me, and a tear trickled down my cheek.

"Hey, don't get upset," Misty said. "It was six years ago now. Time's helped to heal things. And so has Archie. I know everyone thinks we're crazy for getting married so soon, but we believe in each other."

"Sometimes you just know, right?"

Dammit, I didn't even have a sleeve to wipe my face with. *Stay upbeat, Imogen.*

"Right."

"You really met playing a video game?"

Now Misty giggled. "A first-person shooter, and I killed him. But then we got talking in the chat room, and right from the first moment, we just clicked. That was fourteen months ago, but people hear the six-weeks thing and don't realise that there's more to a relationship than physicality."

"So you got to know each other over the phone?"

"We called each other all the time. Some nights, I hardly slept. I'd go into work the next day, and the make-up team would bitch like crazy because of the bags under my eyes. Except I thought we'd only ever be friends because, hello, porn actress, and each time Archie suggested meeting, I kept putting him off."

"But you changed your mind?"

"He asked for my address to mail me a gift, then flew to Florida to surprise me on my birthday." She put her hands over her eyes. "I'd only ever sent him photos of me *au naturel,* so I'm not sure who got the bigger shock when I answered the door in full make-up. Hey, how did you and Malachi meet?"

"Uh, through a mutual friend."

There, that sounded so much better than admitting he'd saved me from certain arrest by getting me out of my cheating ex's apartment right before the cops arrived. And I wasn't entirely lying. Our meeting *this* week had been via a mutual friend. Well, more of an acquaintance. I wasn't sure Sofia had friends. Coven sisters, possibly.

"You make a cute couple. Anyone can see how much Malachi cares."

Exactly how much had Misty drunk so far today?

"He's one in a million."

As in, the only one in a million who'd pretend to date me.

"Where is he?"

"Down on the beach. He fell asleep. I was supposed to be getting drinks, but I needed to use the bathroom, and I got lost, and..." I waved at the room with the hand that wasn't holding the remains of my bikini together. "This happened."

"I'm so sorry."

"Isn't that my line?"

Now we both laughed, and I understood why Archie had gone crazy over this girl. She was lovely.

"I have spare bikinis," she offered. "But they're all white or cream."

"I've actually got another one with me, but it's in my bag, and that's on the beach with Malachi."

"Could you call him? Ask him to bring it?"

"My phone's in my bag too, and I don't know his number by heart."

"Then let me find you a robe or something. At least that way you'll be able to walk around without looking like an extra from one of my movies."

"I've never been to a wedding in a bikini before."

"Me neither. But the wedding was so last-minute, and I felt guilty at the thought of everyone rushing around buying expensive dresses. And we have the beach, and the pool... All I wanted was a relaxed, chilled-out day." She laid a hand on my arm. "What happened totally wasn't your fault."

Upstairs, Misty led me into a luxuriously appointed room dominated by a four-poster bed. The floor-to-ceiling windows opened onto a balcony overlooking the beach, and I could make out the tiny figure of Malachi, still flat-out on the sand.

"Who does this house belong to? Does somebody actually live here?"

"Joey Sambuco." She must have seen my blank look. "Uncle Joey?"

"Uh, I don't know who that is."

She gave a throaty chuckle, dirtier than her giggles downstairs. "Guess you're a good girl."

I nearly choked. "Not many people would describe me that way."

"Well, you don't watch a lot of porn. Joey's, like, a legend."

Okay, I'd give her that. After years of working in the sex industry, the last thing I wanted to do when I got home was to watch other people having sex. For me, it was a tool. First, I'd sold myself out of need, and then when I quit Rubies, I offered myself up in the forlorn hope that it might lead to more. Now? Now I was on the verge of swapping my panties out for a chastity belt or perhaps investing in a games console.

Unless, of course, my dastardly plan to snag Jean-Luc worked.

"Porn's never really been my thing. Not that I've got anything against it. I mean, it's totally up to you what you choose to do for work."

"If only everyone thought that way. I've had everything from death threats to old ladies offering up prayers to save my soul from eternal damnation. Yes, there's a seedy side to the industry, but we're not all being exploited." She opened an ornate closet on the far side of the room and held up a cream silk dressing gown for me to slip my arms into. "Here you go. Uh, you might want to take a look at your face too. Erin smeared your mascara."

Great. "Thanks."

"There's a bathroom right over there. Use whatever you want."

Smeared my mascara? When I looked in the bathroom mirror, I realised I'd turned into a freaking raccoon. Once I'd done what I originally came inside for, I set about fixing the mess. Uncle Joey—and don't even get me started on how creepy that moniker was—sure kept his bathrooms well-stocked. The drawers of the vanity overflowed with high-end cosmetics and expensive face creams, most of them unopened. We never got perks like that from Rubies.

My heart rate still hadn't quite calmed down from

earlier. How was I supposed to explain to Malachi that I'd been in a catfight with his ex? He'd brought me here because he wanted to avoid drama, not get a hand in creating it. Should I confess all? Pretend nothing happened and that I broke my nail opening a door? What if I kept quiet and Misty told everyone? Or those two guys...the bouncers... What were their names?

By the time I'd decided that telling the truth was the best course of action, Misty had disappeared. Excellent. Now I had to find my way out of this stupid mansion, and all the doors looked the same. Had I already been that way before?

Finally, I managed to find a staircase and get back to the first floor. If all else failed, I could climb out the window now, at least, I could if I found one that didn't open onto shrubbery. Where was everyone? The house had suddenly turned into the Marie Celeste.

Footsteps approached from behind, soft, the quiet squeak of rubber on tile. Hurrah—I could ask for help.

Except before I could turn around, I felt the most awful pain in my shoulder, a stinging, pricking sensation as if I'd been punched forward by a monster wearing spiked leather gloves. I tried to scream, but no sound came out, and my knees gave way.

"Wha... *What*...?"

I wanted to form sentences, but my brain wouldn't talk nicely to my mouth. What was going on?

A shadow fell over me, long and dark, and I couldn't see the owner's face, only the outline of what he carried in his hand. A syringe. I was helpless to resist as he jerked down my robe then stabbed the needle into my shoulder again.

What...? Who...? *Why*...? I wanted answers, but I

couldn't even keep my eyelids open.
Then everything faded to black.

Chapter 11 - Malachi

MALACHI BANKS HAD a small problem. Well, not that small if the copy of Erin's *Cosmopolitan* he'd borrowed to read on the shitter one morning was to be believed. About eight and a half inches. Measuring was normal, okay? Every man did it.

And that eight and a half inches had dug into the sand like an inverse totem pole when Imogen straddled him.

Yeah, pretending to be asleep was a cowardly thing to do, but if he rolled over in a pair of swim shorts, his loss of control would be all too evident, not least to Imogen herself. And this was supposed to be a business arrangement.

"There, all done," Imogen said.

The lady had magic fucking hands. Hands that rightfully belonged to another man. Some French chef who made desserts for a living as opposed to getting shot at and breaking into buildings deemed as secure as Fort Knox.

But damn, Imogen was beautiful. The first time Mal met her, he'd still been dating Erin, and he may have been an asshole in many ways, but he wasn't a cheat. So he'd taken Imogen back to her apartment, checked the place over, then walked away. But he'd never forgotten her.

Back then, she'd been bubbly, vivacious, and by reputation—he'd asked around—a man-eater. The kind of girl guys viewed either as a challenge to be conquered or as a difficulty to be avoided altogether. And now? Now that Mal had spent more time with her, he detected a hint of something else lurking under the confident exterior. Sadness? Fear? A little bit of both? One thing was certain—the combination meant trouble.

Don't think about the hands, asshole.

"I'm gonna go and get a drink," she said. "Do you want anything?"

Other than a jug of iced water to pour over his dick?

"Malachi?"

He stayed silent. Sensed rather than saw her walk away

By feigning sleep, Mal hoped Erin would steer clear of him too. Getting tangled up with that banshee had been the biggest mistake of his life. She'd seemed so normal when they met at one of Archie's parties, a statuesque redhead who wasn't afraid to make the first move.

Pre-Erin, Mal had been more of a one-night stand kind of a guy. With the unpredictable hours he worked, finding a long-term girlfriend had been the last thing on his mind, but when she'd called him and put in the effort he didn't have time to make, falling into a relationship with her had been easy. Too bad she turned out to be a head case, as Emmy put it.

Five minutes passed. Ten, and Mal ran through his schedule for the week in his mind. Monday morning— go to the gym, then attend a strategy meeting for a new project. He'd spend an hour after lunch on the shooting range, and his colleague Logan had come up with a new hostage rescue simulation that everybody on the Special Projects team had to run through at least once. Tuesday, he had a defensive driving refresher session, and Wednesday they were supposed to be jumping out of an airplane. The Special Projects team trained *a lot*. Being a special-ops commando in what was essentially a small, elite private army took work. The more they bled in training, the less they'd bleed in battle, that was Emmy's philosophy. Although on Thursday, he was signed up for another first aid course, just in case.

He flexed his hips a little, testing progress with his dick. Still semi-hard. What was he meant to be doing on Friday?

Fifteen minutes passed. Or was it twenty? Where was Imogen? Mal propped himself up on his elbows and scanned the grounds, but she was nowhere in sight. And he'd spot her anywhere.

Had she stopped to talk to the bartender? Mal felt a stab of jealousy at the thought, completely irrational, but that didn't prevent him from rising to his feet, brushing the sand off himself, and heading in that direction.

"Keep an eye on my girl's bag, would ya?" he called to a nearby security guard.

"Sure thing."

Imogen had already made one mistake in the last week from getting too friendly with a stranger, and Mal didn't want to see her make another. Except as he approached the table, the bartender waved at him. If Mal had to put money on it, he'd guess the guy was a colleague of Misty's, moonlighting for extra cash.

"Hey! Your girlfriend forgot to pick up her drink. It's getting warm. Should I add more ice?"

"Did you see where she went?"

"Up to the main house to use the bathroom."

Casa di Amore was a lemon-yellow eyesore belonging to Joseph Smithson, AKA Joey Sambuco, owner of one of the world's best-known porn networks. Mal had gotten curious and looked the man up after Archie told him where the wedding was being held. He may also have been familiar with some of Sambuco's movies, but that was perfectly normal, okay? Every guy watched porn, and those that said they didn't were lying.

What the house lacked in taste, it made up for in size, an observation that could equally be applied to Joey's business empire. Had Imogen gotten lost inside the monstrosity?

He was about to try navigating the maze himself when Misty walked out of a door onto the terrace. She'd swapped out the veil for a tiara, but her smile sparkled more.

"Hey, did Imogen find you?" she asked.

"Was she looking? I fell asleep on the beach."

"Oh. I... She... Uh..."

"Did something happen?"

"Um..."

"Tell me."

"There was an altercation with Erin. Imogen wasn't really hurt, I don't think, just a broken nail and some scratches on her back, but Erin pulled her bikini apart. I lent her a robe, and she borrowed my bathroom to freshen up, but I stepped outside for a second to speak to the band, and when I got back, she was gone. She didn't go to find you?"

"They got into a fight?"

"Only a small one."

"Where's Erin now?"

"Gone. I had her thrown out. I don't know what I'm gonna tell Archie, but she was snorting coke in the freaking dining room, so I couldn't let her stay."

Ah, fuck. Drugs were just one of Erin's many, many issues. Mal had tried to convince her to quit, even offered to pay for rehab, but Erin had refused to accept she had a problem. Finally, he'd admitted defeat. He couldn't take the substance abuse or the unreasonable demands or the mood swings any longer. He'd got sick of walking around on eggshells in his own damn home.

But *she'd* ditched *him*, believe it or not. In the middle of a stand-up row in her kitchen, she'd threatened him with a knife then screamed bloody murder when he'd disarmed her.

"Get off! Get off! It's over, do you understand? Don't you dare touch me! Get out of my apartment."

As he left, all he felt was a sense of relief. Why had he put up with her insanity for so long? At first, it was the sex, then he thought he could help her, but in the end... It just became normal.

She'd called a day later and tried to apologise, but by then, he'd had a night to sleep on things and stuck to his guns. They were done. He should have dumped her ass after she screwed a colleague of hers in New York, an incident he found out about when the guy tagged her on fucking Facebook and Archie noticed, but she'd promised she'd change. She didn't. Nor did her indiscretions stop her from telling everyone she knew that Mal had hurt her in the struggle, bruised her wrists, and that now he was begging her to give him a second chance.

This was what he'd walked Imogen into, using her as a human shield, and now he regretted ever agreeing to Sofia's stupid plan.

"I'll talk to Archie, but I need to look for Imogen first," Mal told Misty. "Any idea where she went?"

"Sorry. I thought she'd wait for me and we'd walk out together. She's nice. Must be a breath of fresh air after Erin, if you don't mind me saying."

"No, I don't mind, but I need to find her." Mal pulled his phone out of his pocket, but before he could dial, Misty shook her head.

"Imogen didn't have her phone. She said it was in her bag on the beach with her spare bikini. Probably she went to get it."

That made sense. Except when Mal walked back down to the beach, Imogen's pink-and-white striped bag was still there, and there was no sign of her. He spent an hour walking around the house and grounds, speaking to everyone from the waiting staff to the other guests to the band, but nobody else had seen her either. Where the hell had she gone? Could she have snuck off the property? The security guards swore she hadn't walked past, but they didn't seem all that switched-on. Although where would she have gone wearing a silk robe with her wallet and phone still in the bag in Mal's hand?

He'd messaged Oliver to ask Stefanie if Imogen had been in touch, just in case she'd borrowed a phone, but the answer came back negative. How could a girl just vanish from a wedding reception full of people?

Misty waved to get Mal's attention. "Any sign of her?"

The band had struck up out on the terrace, and she

was dancing, but she asked the same question every time he walked past.

"Nothing. How upset was she?"

"Honestly, she looked okay. A few tears, but that seemed to be shock more than anything else. I'd never have left her alone if I was worried. Could she have fallen down somewhere, do you think?"

An older man with a hairline too perfect to be natural sauntered over to join them. He had to be at least sixty, but he wore swim shorts and still had a faint six-pack. Joey Sambuco, if Mal wasn't mistaken.

"Is there a problem here?"

"Malachi's date's gone missing," Misty said.

"Too much champagne?" Joey suggested.

"I don't think so. She had an argument with Erin right before she vanished. You know, the red-haired bridesmaid?"

"The one I said was trouble?"

"Yes."

Joey gave his head a faint shake. "Worked with thousands of girls, and I can spot the problems from a mile away. You think Erin scared her off?"

"Maybe."

"Do the cameras at your gates record?" Mal asked. "I want to work out whether she left the property."

"Sure, we can review the tapes."

"Do you want me to help?" Misty asked. "Or should we organise a search party?"

Fuck, this was her wedding. She should have been saving everyone from Archie's dad-dancing, not hunting for a missing woman. Mal forced a smile.

"No, you go take care of Archie. I'm sure there's a simple explanation for all of this."

Inside, Mal followed Joey through the ornate hallways, the older man moving with surprising haste. A few shards of shattered glass on the floor made him *tsk-tsk-tsk*. There had been more earlier when Mal walked the same way, and whoever cleared the mess up hadn't done a very good job.

"Thanks for helping with this," Mal said.

"Number one rule in my business: always look after the girls."

"Have you known Misty a long time?"

"She made her first movie with me. I knew right from the start she was special—kind, smart, ambitious... She deserves everything she's got. To tell you the truth, I was worried when she told me she was marrying Archie, but I think he'll be good for her. Too many men who go after the women in this industry are kooks."

Joey's office was on the first floor, overlooking the front driveway and a hideous sculpture of women with their legs open spraying water into a small pool from... Yeah, tasteless didn't even begin to cover it.

A pair of monitors on the other side of the room showed the security camera feeds, and Mal studied them closely. Good quality pictures, no fuzziness.

"Can you start two hours ago? That's when Imogen went inside." Dammit, he should have done this sooner, but he honestly didn't think she'd have left without saying a word.

"Do you want to see the indoor cameras too?"

"You record in here?"

"Only at the doors and the hallway outside this room. Someone stole a copy of an unreleased movie from here during a party once, and it got uploaded onto a bunch of free sites."

"Did you find out who?"

"Yes, but it was too late by then. He won't work in this industry again, but that release was screwed. Your girlfriend's a blonde?"

"About an inch shorter than Misty, but she looks quite similar."

"I think I saw her earlier. Pretty little thing."

Pretty didn't do Imogen justice. Fuck, where was she? If Erin had messed her up...

"This her?" Joey asked as a head of blonde hair came into view wearing a silky cream robe. "Or is that Misty?"

Mal squinted at the screen. Scripted writing on the back of the robe read *Bride*.

"I'm not sure."

Would Misty really have given Imogen her wedding outfit? From what he'd seen of her, she had a generous soul, and he suspected the answer might be yes. On screen, a waiter walked past, head down, pushing a cloth-covered cart filled with empty glasses. A tall guy with a bald spot. Skinny. Mal hadn't spoken to him. Perhaps he should?

Joey spoke softly into his phone, asking Misty about the robe. After a moment, he nodded.

"That was Imogen. Misty felt bad Erin snapped her bikini string."

"Where does this hallway go?" Mal racked his brain from the hunt earlier. "Is there a dining room around the corner?"

"The dining room's on the other side. This hallway leads to the prop room. Spare beds, couches, that sort of thing."

Then what reason did a member of the catering staff have for walking along there? Unless he was as lost as everyone else seemed to be.

Mal kept watching. He expected Imogen to come back once she realised she'd gone in the wrong direction, except she didn't. But the waiter did, still with his head down as if he knew the camera was watching. And he was in a hurry. When he paused to glance behind him, the cart bumped into the wall and a glass fell off, but that wasn't what made Mal's chest seize. No, what made his heart stop was the arm that flopped out from under the white cloth and trailed along the tile.

Tell him that wasn't Imogen.

Except it was. He recognised the bright pink nail polish, and when Joey zoomed in with a trembling hand, Mal could even see one nail was missing as Misty had mentioned earlier.

"Fuck."

"Did... Did that..." Joey swallowed and tried again. "Did that waiter just kidnap a woman from out of my damn house?"

"Sure looks that way."

Mal's heart hammered against his ribcage. He dealt with these kinds of problems all the time for work, but it had never gotten personal like this. Some fucker had stolen his date out from under his nose, and what was more, it'd happened over an hour ago.

This wasn't good.

And worse? Now he needed to explain the situation to his colleagues.

CHAPTER 12 - MALACHI

MALACHI BREATHED INTO the silence on the other end of the phone, biting back curses.

Finally, Cruz spoke. "Are you fucking around?"

"I only wish I was."

"Who the hell took her?"

"We don't know yet. The perp was dressed as a waiter, but the catering staff are all accounted for."

"An impostor?"

"Possibly. He kept his head down, so we don't have a clear shot of his face. The guy who owns the house is calling the catering company."

"I'm on my way. What do you need?"

"A dozen roadblocks an hour ago."

"Tricky. Do you have a vehicle description?"

"He took off in a van, but we don't have the licence number."

Because in Joey Sambuco's life, appearances took priority over security, and he'd told his gardeners not to trim the bushes at the front of the house until they finished flowering. Those blooms had partially obscured the security cameras. Joey had men out there right now, hacking branches back in a spectacular demonstration of shutting the stable door after the horse had bolted.

"We'll find her, amigo. I'll be there in twenty

minutes."

No sooner had Cruz hung up, Mal's phone rang again. Oliver was calling. Fuck.

"I just thought I'd check Imogen's okay. She's still not answering."

Not Oliver. Stefanie. Double fuck.

Should he tell a little fib? Try to soften the blow?

"We're still looking for her at the moment. She had a small argument with my ex, so she might have wanted to keep out of the way for a while."

"You mean she let the opposition win? No way! Imogen never gives in like that. Have you checked all the bathrooms? If she drank too much, she might be feeling ill."

"We're just going to start a more thorough search."

A pause. "What if...? No, that's silly. It couldn't be him."

"Couldn't be who?"

"It doesn't matter. Forget I said anything."

"If Imogen's been having problems with a guy, I need to know."

"He couldn't have followed her there. I mean, she didn't even know she was going herself until yesterday."

"*Who?*"

"I'm not supposed to tell anybody. We have a girl code."

For fuck's sake. "Stefanie, we have reason to believe Imogen might have been abducted. If you know anything that could shed light on who took her, you need to tell me right now."

Stefanie's gasp reminded Mal why he'd avoided mentioning his suspicions in the first place. The last thing he needed was a hysterical female to deal with.

"Abducted? What? How? When? You have to find her! Her brother's deranged."

"You think she's been abducted by her *brother*?"

"He's hated her for years."

"A lot of siblings don't get along, but they don't tend to resort to kidnapping."

"This is different."

"In what way?"

"I'm not meant to talk about it," Stefanie whispered. "I promised."

Could a family member really have tailed Imogen all the way to Florida? They'd flown on a private fucking jet, and they hadn't exactly broadcast where they were going either. The only place they'd spoken about the trip in public was in the bar with Deon, and Mal might have been off-duty that night, but he'd sure as hell have noticed if someone was eavesdropping.

No way.

He'd get to the bottom of the brother story, but it didn't take priority right now.

"Okay. Don't break your promise. Just call me if she contacts you."

"But—"

"I'll keep you updated."

Mal hung up. Time was of the essence, and he didn't want to waste any cajoling Stefanie to give him information that wasn't vital to their cause. Across the room, Joey Sambuco raised an eyebrow expectantly. Mal shook his head. He had his own theory about what had happened to Imogen, and it didn't involve her brother shadowing them halfway across the country. He fired off a quick message to the tech team at

Blackwood, asking them to have a nose around just in case, then focused back on the task at hand.

Time to ask questions.

Misty was in Archie's arms, eyes glistening as she chewed on her bottom lip. And she looked nervous. Fifty bucks said she'd already had the same thought as Mal had. From behind, on that video, even he'd struggled to tell the pair of them apart.

"We need to talk."

She nodded, and Archie's arm tightened around her waist. "It was meant to be me, wasn't it?"

"Do you know who that man was?"

Archie answered for her. "No, but there's no shortage of wackos out there."

"Have there been any direct threats?"

Misty got her voice back. "Since I was on *Horsing Around*—you know, that reality show where celebrities learn to ride horses? After that, everything just stepped up a gear."

"Love letters, death threats, religious nuts determined to save her," Joey said, moving to her elbow in a show of support. "Letters, emails, Facebook messages... One freak broke into her place last year and cooked her dinner."

"And he wasn't a keeper?" Mal asked, trying to lighten the mood.

"He made beef stroganoff, and I'm a vegetarian."

A thought struck him, and he turned to Archie. "Was that what you wanted to ask me about earlier? These problems?"

"I didn't know whether they were something or nothing."

Well, they had their answer now. "Is that why you

hired security for today?"

"I just wanted everything to go without a hitch. Well, obviously I was getting hitched, but you know what I mean."

"I do."

"And it's also partly why I decided to take a step back from acting," Misty said. "Nobody remembers who's behind the camera. I've been thinking about focusing on directing for a while now, and meeting Archie gave me the push I needed."

"We'll need to look into the threats. Anything recent, anything that mentions violence or kidnapping. Can you help us with access?"

"Whatever you need. Should I send all the guests home? Call the police?"

"Yes, we should call the police." In a situation like this, extra manpower helped, and the Fort Lauderdale PD had proven to be reasonably competent on similar investigations in the past, just slightly lax with the paperwork. Blackwood could run their own team alongside. "And keep everyone out of the house."

An hour later, Casa di Amore was filled with cops, who nibbled on canapés while they talked to tipsy guests. The best part? Somebody had located Erin and brought her back for questioning.

"Some people stop at nothing to be the centre of attention," she muttered.

"Hello, pot. Have you met kettle?" Mal asked.

"I've never ruined anybody's wedding."

"Actually, you did," Misty pointed out.

"Oh, please. I defended myself. *She* went and got kidnapped."

How the hell had Mal dated this bitch for so long?

"Are you fucking kidding me? Imogen didn't ask to be stuffed into a catering trolley."

"Just leave it," Cruz said, steering him away from Erin before he got tempted to dump her in the ocean. With a concrete block attached to her feet. "She's not worth it, and we have work to do. Several of the houses on this street have cameras on their gates, and I bet at least one caught the van on tape."

"Do you want the east side or the west side?"

"I'll take the east. Let's go."

"Kidnapped?" The lady's hands flew to cheeks that paled under her tan. She had to be at least seventy, with thinning grey hair brushed into waves reminiscent of a forties movie star. "A girl got kidnapped from Joey's house?"

"It looks that way, ma'am."

"But this area's normally so safe. What should I do? My Herbie's away this week, and it's just me and my sister here on our own. What if the perpetrator comes back?"

"That's unlikely. Usually, these people want to get as far away as possible. We know he left in a van, but we don't have a great description, and I see you have a camera on top of your gatepost."

"Are you with the police?"

"No, my name's Malachi Banks, and I'm with Blackwood Security. We're looking into the case. I have

ID right here, and you're welcome to call the office for verification."

"Did Joey hire you?"

"Not formally. I was a guest at the wedding that's going on over there."

"Misty's wedding?"

"That's right."

"Such a sweet girl. She invited me, but my sister's recovering from a broken hip, and I didn't want to leave her on her own."

"You know Misty?"

"Oh, yes. Every Christmas, Joey has a big party, and Misty's always there. She bought one of my Herb's paintings. He's an artist, you know."

"Do you think I could check your camera footage?"

"Let me just call Joey. A gal can never be too careful. I'm Lindy, by the way."

Two minutes later, Mal got ushered into the living room with an offer of coffee, whisky, or anything else he wanted. Apart from a smoothie—those were an overpriced con, according to Lindy. Not a health freak, then, and Mal detected the faint aroma of marijuana lingering in the air.

Giant canvases dominated the room—nudes painted in garish colours, broad brush strokes and splashes that looked careless but which were probably placed with excruciating precision. The signature in the corner read F Herbert. The work of Lindy's artist husband? No wonder she'd been so laid back about Joey living across the road.

"I'm actually in a hurry, ma'am. The cameras?"

"My Herbie installed those. I don't really know how they work."

"Could I take a look?"

"All the electronic doohickeys are in his study."

It wasn't a bad system, but whoever installed it had angled the cameras badly. Rather than covering the house and driveway, the one on the gatepost looked straight down the road. Not so good for home security, but great for Mal. The licence plate showed for a clear second as the van drove away from the property, and the vehicle also had a large dent in the rear door, rusty around the edges as if the driver had reversed into a post at some point and never gotten the damage repaired.

"Is that it?" Lindy asked.

"Sure looks like it." The driver wasn't much more than a dark silhouette, but Mack, one of the technical gurus at head office, could enhance that. "Do you mind if I take a copy?"

"Take whatever you want. That poor girl."

Mal's heart stuttered again. Usually, it was easy to stay detached, some might say cold, but all he could think about today was Imogen's smile when she'd climbed on board the jet earlier. Even though the trip to Florida promised to be anything but fun, she'd still been happy. A breath of fresh air. In the same situation, Erin would have found something to complain about for sure.

If they got Imogen back, Mal had a lot of making up to do. When. *When* they got her back. He had to stay positive. Statistically speaking, most victims of abduction came back home. *But eighty-five percent of those who didn't were murdered within the first three hours.* Fuck. Imogen had been gone for two hours already. Thinking about statistics was a bad idea.

Just focus on the clues, Malachi. Not the woman.

Chapter 13 - Malachi

MACK WORKED QUICKLY. Within ten minutes, Mal and Cruz had an address for Morton Seacroft, a thirty-four-year-old Fort Lauderdale resident with no criminal history. His last known residence was just nine miles from Casa di Amore.

As the pair of them drove towards his house in Cruz's Jeep, the updates came thick and fast.

"According to his LinkedIn profile, Seacroft worked at Make a Splash Food & Events until May of this year," Cruz said. "Weren't they the caterers at the wedding?"

"Yes. Joey Sambuco said he always used them."

"So perhaps Seacroft saw Misty at a previous party and took a shine to her?"

"That's possible. Can we send somebody over to speak to the boss? Joey called him, but one of our people needs to ask questions too."

Cruz was already on the phone to Blackwood's Florida office. "I'll sort that out."

"I've got a satellite image of Seacroft's house," Mack said. "Sending it over now. The place is small, but there's a garage at the back."

A garage Mal found himself watching from the other side of a rickety fence an hour later with Cruz crouched beside him. The whole property was unkempt, overgrown, and the garage roof sagged in the middle. Worse, there were no signs of life, and the driveway was empty.

"Nobody's home," Cruz said.

"The question is, has he abandoned the place completely?"

They already knew he rented. The landlord said he'd been there for almost two years, no trouble apart from paying late on occasion. One of Mack's assistants had called pretending to need a reference. The same assistant had also been tasked with looking at Imogen's brother but hadn't yet managed to find any trace of the man. Or, strangely, any trace of Imogen herself before she moved to Richmond. Mal vowed to follow up on that later, but at that moment, there were more important things to do, such as searching Morton Seacroft's residence.

"Only one way to find out," Cruz said. "Do you want to go in, or shall I?"

Cruz was an investigator, a former police detective who'd seen the light rather than ex-military like many of Blackwood's employees. He wouldn't be so good in a fight, but he was observant, and that was what Mal needed right now.

"I'll go in. You keep watch and check out the garage."

Keep watch not just for their suspect's return but for the cops too. Blackwood hadn't yet mentioned this latest development to the Fort Lauderdale PD because Mal wanted to check out the house without having to iron out pesky details such as getting a search warrant first. But the police were running their own investigation, albeit a slower, more cumbersome one, and it wouldn't be long before they found Seacroft's address too.

And if the asshole happened to arrive back? Mal would take him down the instant he stepped out of his damn vehicle. Cruz carried the essentials in his trunk— rope, duct tape, handcuffs—and if Imogen wasn't in the van, Mal was good at extracting information. Emmy had a training course for everything. *Getting men to talk 101* was run by an old friend of hers, a former Mossad agent who'd taught Mal a dozen creative ways to use a nine-volt battery. Cruz had one of those with him too.

Mal pulled on a pair of thin leather gloves and slipped forward into the shadows. They were already miked up, which meant they could communicate not only with each other but with the Blackwood control room back in Richmond. Nate, one of Blackwood's directors, had designed the system, and speaking across three states was as clear as talking across the room.

"Not much of a lock," Mal muttered, picking a bump key from his set. Ten seconds later, he was inside.

The house was tidier than he'd expected, almost spartan. A bedroom, a combined living room/dining area/kitchenette, and a tiny bathroom, the furniture old and threadbare but clean. The home of a neat freak without much money by the look of things. Two things interested Mal. Firstly, the computer on a desk by the window. A bulky old model, but the green light flashing on the front showed it still worked. Secondly, there was a pair of ladies' slippers beside the bed and a pink bathrobe hanging beside the white one on the back of the bathroom door. Toiletries no self-respecting man would use—lilac and apple blossom shampoo and conditioner, peach face wash, and moisturiser that promised to leave your legs silky smooth—were lined up beside the sink. Every bottle was full.

Did a woman live here too? A girlfriend? Or...?

A shelf in the closet was stacked with men's clothes —well-worn jeans, T-shirts, and underwear that had seen better days. But the rail underneath held women's garments. Pretty dresses, skirts, and blouses, all with the tags on.

Expensive chocolates sat beside the cans of SpaghettiOs in the kitchen cupboard. Scented candles in plastic wrappers nestled in an old wooden blanket box right beside three new-looking romance novels and a foot spa.

No, Seacroft didn't have a girlfriend. He *wanted* a girlfriend. This was his fantasy.

"Nothing in the garage," Cruz said in Mal's ear. "Unless you count spiders. There's a lot of spiders. And judging by the tyre marks, he usually parks the van in there."

"It's not set up to hold a prisoner?"

"There's a man-sized hole in the back wall."

Back to the computer. It whirred away, left on as if Seacroft had either high-tailed it out of the house in a hurry or expected to return soon. Or perhaps he was just lazy? When Mal nudged the mouse, it asked for a password. He hadn't honestly expected anything else, but to see the cursor there flashing at him was still a disappointment. Thankfully, Blackwood planned ahead for these little problems. Mal plugged in an external hard drive already loaded with Mack's proprietary software, and as Seacroft's secrets began copying across, he got back to his search of the house.

Not much food in the fridge, and nothing that expired in the next week. Seacroft hadn't written anything on his calendar past March. Get a haircut. Mow the lawn. Buy laundry detergent. The gym dates had fizzled out in January. Nothing about abducting an adult movie star.

Boy, this guy really knew how to live.

How long to go on the disc? Eighty percent done. Mal had a more thorough hunt for hiding places while he waited—the usual spots like in the toilet tank and beneath the mattress. Nothing. No loose floorboards either that he could see. Then he found the empty pistol box at the back of the closet and cursed under his breath. Somewhere out there, Seacroft was running around with a Smith & Wesson Model 64 in .38 Special. Not a bad gun, Mal had to concede, but if the fucker pointed it anywhere near Imogen, he'd have to die.

"He threw half a carton of milk in the trash," Cruz said, slipping in through the front door but staying near the window. "Guess he didn't want it to spoil while he played kidnapper."

"Anything else in there?"

"One of those plastic garment covers from the dry cleaner, and the tag from a new shirt. White with pink stripes. And he tossed out his porn magazines."

"He was planning to bring Misty back here. The house is full of girl stuff, all new, ready and waiting."

"Why'd he change his mind?"

"Perhaps because he realised Imogen isn't Misty? The question is, what will he do now?"

"Dump her?" Cruz suggested. "Or try to act out his

sick little fantasy with a different leading lady?"

If he dumped Imogen, would she be alive or dead? For the first time in a decade, Mal felt panic welling up in his stomach. A familiar sensation, but one notable for its absence in the years since he met Emmy and Black. They'd taken his fear and replaced it with determination, and now he forced his training to the fore.

"He's a dead man walking."

"Driving, more likely." Cruz flipped through the papers on the desk. "If he bought Misty clothes, that suggests a certain amount of care. And Imogen looks like her. Harming her would be difficult for him."

Mal wanted to believe that. *Had* to believe that.

"Buddy, I hope you're right."

CHAPTER 14 - MALACHI

"VIVA LAS VEGAS," Mack said, in her smooth southern drawl.

"Vegas?"

"That's what Seacroft was researching in the days before he took Imogen. Directions, hotels, the best places to eat, and, uh, wedding venues."

"Wedding venues? What the fuck?"

"And Seacroft's been sending messages to Misty for months. Years. They started off innocuous, just the ramblings of an obsessed fan, but after she announced her engagement, he wrote her fifty times a day telling her she'd chosen the wrong man. Oh, and he calls himself her fiancé."

Cruz was sitting next to Mal in the Jeep, which was parked in the driveway outside Casa di Amore. Joey had offered them a bed for the night, and while Mal could have borrowed Cruz's spare room, he preferred to stay in the middle of things. Not that he could sleep, anyway.

"The wedding tipped him over the edge, didn't it?" Cruz said. "Finding out Misty was betrothed to another man."

"Betrothed?" Mal asked. "What century are you living in?"

"And he planned to take her to Vegas and walk her

down the aisle before they came back to Florida to play happy families. What was he gonna do? Brainwash her into saying 'I do'?"

Mal thought back to the empty pistol box. "I don't think he's got that much finesse."

"And Misty said he always seemed so quiet."

Yes, when they showed her the photo from his driver's licence, she'd recognised him from Joey's parties. The first time she met him, he'd dropped a tray of champagne all over the terrace, and she'd stepped in when his supervisor tried to fire him on the spot. Accidents happened, she said, and after that, he always kept her glass topped up. Their conversations had been nothing more than small talk, but clearly they'd meant more to Seacroft than they did to Misty.

According to his former boss, Seacroft had kept to himself, turned up on time, and always spoke politely to clients. Apart from the champagne mishap, he'd been a model employee, but he quit after an internal reshuffle left him waiting at corporate events rather than private parties.

Funny what made a man lose his mind.

Or who.

Having met Imogen, Mal could almost understand it.

"We need to find them, and fast. He lacks sophistication, but he's got plenty of options. Vegas might have been his original plan, but thanks to the mix-up at the wedding reception, he's deviated. How will he handle that?"

Cruz ticked off the possibilities on his fingers.

"One, he drops Imogen off at a gas station and pretends this never happened. Maybe he makes another play for Misty. Two, he gets rid of the evidence." Cruz refused to look at Mal when he said that. "Three, he tries to shoehorn Imogen into Misty's place."

"So basically, we have to search from the Everglades to the Mojave Desert while we pray for a phone call. Even if we got the whole of Blackwood involved, that's still an impossible task."

"The Fort Lauderdale PD can handle the basic legwork here, and we'll crib off their notes. We're already rearranging workloads in the office. How many people can we bring in from elsewhere? Mack?"

"I'll ask the scheduling team," Mack said. "And I'll also contact the Vegas office. They can start calling around the hotels I've found in the search history. But when Seacroft gets to the city, there are so many places to hide. If he *is* heading to Vegas, it'd be a hundred times easier if we stopped him before the city limits."

How long would it take Seacroft to get to Nevada? Two days? Maybe more if he stopped overnight to rest. But he had a twelve-hour head start, and Mal hadn't gotten any sleep either.

Should he head west? If Imogen was still in the Florida area, the police stood a good chance of finding her now that their wheels had ground into motion, especially with Blackwood providing assistance as well as running their parallel investigation. But what if a rescue was needed on the other side of the country? Mal rated his own chances as better than local law enforcement's.

"How the hell do we find one van on two-and-a-half thousand miles of roads? Can you do anything with cameras?"

"Not in this country. There's not much of a network."

"Satellites?"

"Too slow to manoeuvre into position. But you know who's on the west coast at the moment?"

From the way Mack said it, Mal dreaded to think. "Who?"

"Emmy. You should call her. You know how much she loves solving impossible problems."

Yeah, and she'd also make sure he never lived this one down. Letting his date get kidnapped from right in front of him? Mal could hear the laughter now. Plus Emmy would tell Sofia what had happened, and he might wake up castrated.

But he swallowed his pride.

"Okay, I'll call her."

CHAPTER 15 - EMMY

EMMY BLACK ADJUSTED her sunglasses and turned to the next page of her book. Okay, so it was actually a gun catalogue, but it was still words on paper. She'd started off reading a biography of President James Harrison, but the number of factual inaccuracies was stunning and she'd tossed it into the ocean an hour earlier. Then fished it back out again in case a dolphin choked on it.

"Sure you don't want to join us?" her husband asked, pausing next to her to knock back the rest of his smoothie. Whatever he'd put in it, it smelled worse than the stomach contents she'd vomited up in the early hours of the morning. Trying to match two former Navy men in the drinking stakes hadn't gone well.

"I'm sure."

"Lightweight."

"Fuck you."

He just laughed and jogged back towards the water. Asshole.

Usually when they came to California, they stayed in their own beach house in Malibu, but since they had work to do in San Diego this time, Black had suggested staying with an old friend of his so they could catch up. And by catch up, he meant plan a murder and go surfing. The target was dead, hence last night's celebrations, and now the two men were out on longboards while Emmy recovered.

Pale's house was out in the sticks between Oceanside and San Clemente. Two storeys, six bedrooms, seven bathrooms, eighteen acres, and a private beach. Far too big for one man, but Pale liked his space and his privacy, much the same as Black did. They'd been buddies for years, going back to their days in the Navy SEALs followed by a stint in a shadowy CIA unit Black rarely talked about. There'd been four men in their team, nicknamed the four horsemen. White had died on active duty, something that led the remaining three members to re-evaluate their priorities. For Black, that meant regaining control. He didn't like being told what to do, especially by asshole politicians who played God from behind a desk, so he'd started Blackwood Security with Red, also known as Nate Wood. And Pale? He'd moved to Hawaii and funded his surfing habit with the occasional contract killing.

But now Pale was back.

Partly due to boredom, Emmy suspected, but mostly because of one more tragic death. Another old friend of his, gone, and not even on a job this time. No, he'd pulled over at the side of the highway with car trouble, only to get shunted a hundred yards by a semi whose driver got distracted on the phone.

That friend had been running a top-secret project training the latest batch of government assassins how to do the impossible. Emmy's competition, Pale called them, but she disagreed. With all the shit going on in the world, there was plenty of work for everyone, plus she'd been trained by Black. Pale was good, but Black was better.

Anyhow, the powers that be had wheedled, cajoled, and finally offered Pale a fuck ton of cash to take charge of the Choir. Now, he'd confessed last night, he was being driven mad by eight women who scattered make-up all over his Vegas home, used his ammo, and nagged him when he left the toilet seat up. He was only too glad to come to California for a break.

Pale crested a wave on his longboard as Black paddled out to sea. Both men were shirtless, and Emmy had to admit she was enjoying the view. Yes, there were worse ways to spend a Monday morning, and she and Black had earned half a million bucks for yesterday's job. They deserved a day off.

Then the phone rang.

Ah well, the peace was nice while it lasted. What did Malachi want? A tiny knot tightened in Emmy's stomach because last year when he'd surprised her with an unexpected call, he'd accidentally foiled a diamond heist in France while on a totally unrelated surveillance trip, and although the outcome had been satisfying—Blackwood three, robbers nil—the car chase through the streets of Paris had gotten messy.

"Everything okay?"

"There's a small problem."

"How small?"

"About a hundred and forty pounds."

"Go on."

"Imogen got kidnapped from the wedding we went to."

"Could you repeat that? For a moment, I thought you said your fake date got kidnapped."

"She went to use the bathroom, okay?"

Emmy tried not to laugh. Really she did. But Mal walked through danger every day at work, only for disaster to strike on his vacation.

"It's not funny."

"I know. Honestly, I know. I might still be a tiny bit drunk from last night."

Mal muttered a few curses, and Emmy couldn't blame him for that. "We think he might be headed west for Las Vegas. Mack got into the suspect's computer, and he's been looking up directions and wedding packages."

"He wants to *marry* Imogen?"

"No, he wants to marry Misty—the girl my friend just tied the knot with. He took Imogen by mistake. They look the same from behind, plus Imogen borrowed Misty's clothes after she got into a catfight with Erin."

"A catfight?" The giggles came back. *Tact, Emmy.* "I don't know why you haven't just pushed Erin out of a plane over the Atlantic. I even offered to lend you a jet."

"Because I thought she'd give up if she saw me with another woman."

"Women like Erin don't give up. They just get crazier. Now, tell me the whole story. Start to finish. What are we dealing with here?"

Mal gave a detailed account, and fuck, Seacroft was delusional from the sound of it. What kind of moron decided to stuff a woman into the back of a van as a form of courtship? Unless she was either threatened or very, very drunk, there was no way Imogen would agree to walk down the aisle, and resistance would only put her in more danger.

And Mal's assessment made sense. Three options.

Either Seacroft was lying low in Florida, or Imogen was lying in a ditch, or the pair of them were somewhere on...fuck, what roads went from Fort Lauderdale to Las Vegas? I-10? I-40?

"Get Cruz to handle the Florida end. He's perfectly capable, and his police connections are better than yours. I'll approve whatever manpower you need." Imogen was a friend of Stefanie's, and Stefanie was Blackwood family. "You can come and help at this end. That'll be the challenging part."

"How the fuck do we find the van?"

"I'll sleep on it."

"Sleep?"

Emmy swallowed a yawn. "Figure of speech. Get your ass in the damn jet, Banks."

So much for having a day off.

Would Seacroft really have chosen to bring Imogen to Las Vegas? Emmy reckoned it was fifty-fifty, but half-hearted operations had little chance of succeeding. Therefore, she'd put a hundred percent of her small team's effort into that fifty percent while the police and the larger Blackwood team did the same with the Florida option.

She opened the maps app on her phone. Yes, Seacroft could've decided to take the scenic route across the country, but the more stops he made, the higher the risk of something going wrong. He wouldn't want to risk losing his prize.

There were three main routes. Fastest would be to take I-10 to Pensacola, then go through Jackson, Shreveport, past Fort Worth, and across to Amarillo. The second route went up to Atlanta, then through Birmingham, Memphis, and Oklahoma City. Finally, he could take I-10 to start with, but turn south from Mobile and travel through Baton Rouge, Houston, El Paso, Tucson, and Phoenix.

Whichever way he chose, he'd have to join I-40 east of Kingman then take Route 93 up to Vegas. A distance of a hundred miles, give or take. That looked like the best place to find him. How long did they have before he got there? Emmy did some rough calculations in her head and figured on fifteen hours minimum. Probably more because he'd have to stop to take a leak at least.

"What's up?" Black asked, leaning over her. "Did you pick out a new toy?"

"Imogen got kidnapped, and you're dripping on me."

Black shook his head, sending a shower of water droplets everywhere. "Sorry." No, he wasn't. "Kidnapped? I thought Malachi was taking her to a wedding?"

"He did. One of the waiters turned out to be a nutter."

"So what's the plan? I take it we're looking for her?"

"He thinks they might be heading for Las Vegas. I need to organise surveillance along Route 93, plus plan a takedown. The problem is, if he rolls into town when I think he might, it'll be dark."

Pale strode up with a surfboard under his arm, and since he had beach-bum hair, that meant even more water.

"Is there a problem? The kid's got his thinking face on."

"I'm only six months younger than you, dickhead," Black said. "And yes, there's a problem. An acquaintance of ours has been kidnapped. We need to leave."

Pale peered down at Emmy's phone. "And she's in Las Vegas?"

"Possibly heading that way."

"Well, so am I. I need to be back there by tonight, so we can take my plane. You can fill me in on the trip."

CHAPTER 16 - EMMY

PALE FLEW A four-seater Mooney Acclaim Ultra he kept at a small airfield near his home. A nice little plane —agile, fast, and comfortable. They flew east as Malachi travelled west on board one of Black's jets. Emmy had spoken to Mal just before they took off, and while he sounded outwardly calm, there was an edge to his voice. A tension that was never normally there, no matter how much shit hit the fan.

Hmm...

Could it be possible that Mal had a crush on a girl who wasn't a raving lunatic? They could but hope. Somebody was going to do jail time if he hooked up with another Erin.

"What's the range on this?" Black asked as they approached the runway at Creech Air Force Base.

"Eight hundred and thirty nautical miles at high speed, twelve hundred and seventy-five cruising."

"We don't need another plane," Emmy told him.

"I know we don't *need* another plane..."

"You can only fly one at a time."

"And that's why you have three cars in Richmond alone?"

Okay, so Emmy had given in and bought another Aston Martin to go with her Dodge Viper and her Corvette Stingray. But the DB11 looked so pretty sitting next to them in the garage.

"The Aston reminds me of home. Buy British and all that."

"Mooney's American, so following your logic..."

"Technically, you're Colombian."

"Technically, you're Russian."

"Half Russian." Which was a touchy subject with Emmy. She hated to be reminded of her roots. "Fine, buy the damn plane."

Black reached back between the seats and squeezed her hand. "Love you, Diamond."

"Whatever."

It was Pale's turn to laugh. "Women are all the same. Never stop talking, and they always have to have the last word." He sighed. "Why did I take this damn job?"

"Is your divorce final yet?" Black asked.

"A month ago. If I ever get drunk and try to marry a stripper again, for fuck's sake, stop me. With a bullet, if necessary."

"Worked out okay for me."

Emmy kicked the back of Black's seat as Pale turned to look at him. The two men didn't have many secrets, but that particular snippet of Emmy's history wasn't common knowledge.

"I meant the getting married while drunk part," he clarified. "What story did you tell her?"

"She may have been under the impression I worked in telesales. I rented a shitty little duplex and everything. Things were okay for three weeks, then she got on my case about earning more commission to pay for her shoe habit."

This was Pale's problem. He never told his wives

the truth about anything, and if you didn't have trust in a marriage, then what was the point? Wife number one, the hula dancer, had thought he was a retired banker, and he'd convinced wife number two, a cocktail waitress, that he was an advertising executive. Apparently, he'd been in love once, real love, but that had ended in tragedy, and ever since, he'd favoured superficial affairs with rings involved. Emmy wasn't supposed to know all of that, of course, but she and Black *did* have trust.

"You deserved everything you got, buddy," he said.

Pale didn't answer, just dropped the landing gear as they descended. Two minutes later, they taxied towards the hangar where his jeep was parked. Welcome to fabulous Las Vegas. The heat was already oppressive, the sun beating down from a clear sky to form a haze in every direction, and Emmy still hadn't worked out how to run airtight surveillance on Route 93 at night. Problems, always problems.

"Where are you going?" Pale asked. "To your hotel?"

Emmy and Black owned the Black Diamond hotel on the strip, and they kept a private apartment on the top floor. Great if Emmy wanted to drink cocktails or play poker, but not so good for planning a security operation.

"Nah, I should head to the office. I've got surveillance to plan. My absolute favourite."

"I've got a better idea for that. Follow me."

Emmy looked at Black, and he shrugged. They followed. First to the jeep, and then into a giant hangar filled with what looked like beige shipping containers on the other side of the base.

"Storm's office," he explained. "You met her in North Carolina, right? That was some police chase."

Ah, yes. The airship debacle of two months ago. Storm had offered up her piloting skills, but she'd muttered something about being shy and disappeared as soon as they landed. Emmy hadn't even had a chance to thank her properly. Storm was based in Las Vegas?

Yes, it seemed, because Pale tapped away at his phone, and a moment later, she appeared at the far end of the hanger, this time wearing jeans and a camisole. Civilian clothes. Was she one of his choir girls?

Again, the answer appeared to be yes, since she saluted. "What's up, boss?"

"We need to find a missing van, and there's a good possibility it's on its way here from Fort Lauderdale with a kidnap victim on board."

"Do you have the description? A registration number?"

"Yeah, we've got the number, and if he's changed the plate, there's also a distinctive dent in the rear door. I'll get a picture sent over." Emmy scribbled the registration details on a flyer she pulled from a nearby noticeboard and passed it over. Weekday special—any two pizzas for the price of one. Great, now she was hungry. "Here you go."

"ETA?"

"The soonest he could get here is about thirteen hours, but it'll be dark."

Storm turned to Pale. "What am I supposed to tell the colonel?"

"I'll handle the colonel. He owes me a favour. Some blonde came over to talk to us in a bar the other day, and when his wife saw and got pissy, I told her she was my girlfriend."

"Why didn't you just tell the truth?" Emmy asked.

"That she was his mistress? I didn't have time for a trip to the emergency room that day."

Okay, fair enough. Emmy had to give him that one.

"How are you gonna find the van?"

Storm grinned, tucking her blonde hair behind her ears. "With unmanned aerial vehicles. Drones. How are your security clearances?"

"They're good," Pale told her.

"Then do you wanna see?"

Definitely. Drones? They were something Emmy hadn't had any experience with, but the technology fascinated her. What were the chances of getting one of those for Blackwood? She'd have to be *very* nice to President Harrison. Black stayed close behind as Storm led them into the furthest container, set up with two ergonomic seats, a bank of screens, and a selection of controllers at the far end. It looked like a cross between a flight simulator and a teenage boy's bedroom, apart from the pair of pink fluffy dice hanging from the ceiling and the orchid sitting in a glass vase beside a mug of coffee. A whiteboard held a tally chart and a note to pick up the dry cleaning.

Emmy pointed at the tally chart. "What's that for?"

"Confirmed kills this month."

"Sixteen." Emmy wasn't sure whether to be worried or impressed. "Congratulations."

"Aw, thanks. But nine of them were in one go. They were having some sort of get-together, and..." She shrugged. "Boom."

"Even so... What kind of drones do you fly here?"

"The regular team flies Reapers. We used to fly the smaller Predators too, but they've been retired."

"Are you part of the regular team?"

"No, I work on testing. They give me the new toys to play with, and I try to break them. This control station is for a Hunter. It's the size of the old Predators, but faster and more agile and with a bigger payload. And most importantly for your task, better optics. This thing'll read a licence plate from twenty thousand feet."

"How many Hunters do you have?"

Storm held up three fingers. "We can fly them above the main roads leading here. If your guy's on his way and he didn't take a detour, we'll find him." Her grin got wider. "And you'll owe me another favour."

Emmy would pay up. She always paid up, even if it half killed her. "Thanks for helping out."

With the surveillance in hand, Emmy and Black headed back to Pale's place since it wasn't too far from the base. He'd gone for a spacious mansion on a two-acre lot this time, and it was a good thing he'd never brought the stripper there or she'd probably have wound up owning it.

Inside, the house smelled of rose with a hint of vanilla. Pale took a deep breath and gritted his teeth.

"Okay, who's been burning scented fucking candles again?"

Nobody answered. The house was silent. Still.

"Abandoned by your harem?" Black asked.

"Shut the fuck up."

Black picked up a pair of curling tongs from the coffee table. Put them down again. Cleared a copy of *Cosmopolitan* and a half-eaten packet of marshmallows off the sofa so he could take a seat.

"Perhaps living with Emmy isn't so bad. She'd have finished the marshmallows."

Emmy unrolled the top of the bag and popped one into her mouth. "Too bloody right. Now, if we do find Seacroft, how are we gonna get him out of his vehicle? Want one?"

She held out the packet to Black, and he turned up his nose in disgust. So did Pale. Did the CIA train them out of eating anything tasty? Oh well, more for her.

Black counted the options on his fingers.

"One, we can cause a crash, but that would put Imogen at risk. If she's riding in the back, she probably isn't wearing a seatbelt. Two, we can give him a reason to pull over—a broken-down car or a staged accident—but there's no guarantee he'll stop to help. Three, we can follow him to his destination and incapacitate him then."

"Three," Pale said. "No question."

Emmy had to concur. "Agreed. Mal reckons Seacroft's got a revolver, so we'll have to be a little careful."

"Do you need more weapons?" Pale asked. "The girls collect guns like they're going out of fashion. I think they enjoy matching them to their outfits. And Dusk's a kleptomaniac. I caught her stowing a surface-to-air missile in the basement last month."

"Do you still have it?"

"Never know when that shit'll come in useful."

"Don't the girls have their own homes to go to?" Black asked.

"In Vegas? Sin's bought a fixer-upper that she hasn't fixed up yet, Storm's got an apartment, and the rest have rooms at Creech. But apparently, my pool's better."

"Sin?"

"Super Intel Nerd. My predecessor gave her the nickname."

"Have you tried locking them out?"

"If you tried locking Emmy out of Riverley, would it work?"

Black laughed. "Sounds like you're fucked. How long's your contract?"

"Another year or until I get committed, whichever comes first."

"Are the girls good at what they do?"

Finally, a sly smile spread over Pale's face. "Oh yeah, they're good. I wouldn't want to get on the wrong side of any of them."

CHAPTER 17 - EMMY

"SALTED PEANUT?"

EMMY offered the packet to Mal, but he shook his head.

"Suit yourself. Did you eat lunch?"

"A protein bar."

Good. He shouldn't be working on a totally empty stomach, although she understood why he wasn't hungry. Having your pretend girlfriend snatched from under your nose was kind of awkward.

"Do you want some water?" Emmy steered with one hand while she used the other to fish around in the door pocket. "I have a bottle."

"I'm good."

"Nah, dude, you're anything but good. Look, shit happens, okay? We all fuck up. Black got kidnapped from under my nose once too, but I got over it." Eventually. It did screw up Emmy's life for the best part of a year. "We'll find her."

"I'm surprised you didn't bring Sofia."

"Sofia's not feeling well."

"She's sick?"

"No, depressed."

"Over what?"

"No idea. Even she doesn't know. I left her at home self-medicating, and Leo's taken the day off work to look after her." Leo was her boyfriend. A nice guy. Not the kind of man Emmy would have imagined her ending up with, but they loved each other. He was a former fitness model, and now they ran a gym together when she wasn't killing people on the side. "But stop changing the subject. We've done loads of jobs like this. Planned, trained, practised... It'll be fine."

"This one's different. I... I like her."

"*Like* her, like her?"

"I think so." He paused for a long moment. "Yeah, I do. She's easy to talk to. Sweet. I already told her about my past, and she seemed to be okay with it."

Well, that was big. Mal usually kept his teenage indiscretions quiet, and as far as I knew, he'd kept Erin in the dark throughout their entire relationship.

"That's good. Isn't it?"

"Too bad everything between us is a pretence," he said.

A pretence, but for how long? If it came down to a choice between Jean-Luc and Malachi, there was no contest.

"Look on the bright side—this'll be over soon. And Imogen's still alive."

"You don't know that for certain."

"Well, I'm ninety-nine percent sure. Seacroft's two hundred miles from Las Vegas. If she was dead, he'd have stopped in the desert to bury the body and then headed home."

Instead of driving merrily along I-40 at sixty-five miles per hour with four cars tailing him and a Hunter UAV flying overhead. Storm's magic drone had spotted Seacroft east of Kingman three hours ago, and the teams had hopped into their vehicles to join him—

Black with Pale, Emmy with Mal, plus two guys from Blackwood's Las Vegas office in a third car and a pair of Pale's girls in a fourth. He'd offered them up in an effort to stop them from rearranging his patio furniture.

They'd headed across to intercept Seacroft, and now they were running a rotating surveillance pattern, taking it in turns to follow behind the van before dropping back to throw off any possible suspicion. As Emmy drove, she daydreamed about shooting out a tyre or jumping across to pry open the back door because just tootling along the highway was getting really boring.

But Imogen took priority, and the safest way to rescue her was to let the asshole stop first. How long until he ran out of gas? Would he make it to the city without refuelling?

No, was the answer.

At two in the morning, he signalled right and pulled into the deserted forecourt of a run-down gas station. Perfect. Two cameras—one mounted on a pole to cover the pumps and the other inside the kiosk by the door, facing the register. Emmy took out the exterior camera with a shot from her silenced .22 before it recorded any of her team. Nobody wanted to be a YouTube star.

The cashier didn't notice, just kept staring at his phone while Pale jammed his Jeep Wrangler in front of the van. The Blackwood car did the same at the rear, and Mal and Black were out and running before Emmy stopped her borrowed Ford Explorer. Pale's girls slewed sideways across the entrance to prevent any unwanted company from joining them.

By the time Emmy got to the van, Black had already

dragged Seacroft onto the concrete and cuffed his hands behind his back, giving Mal enough room to clamber over the seats into the back to help Imogen. The gun and a handful of rounds lay beside a pile of candy wrappers on the passenger seat. Seacroft hadn't even loaded the damn thing? What a bloody idiot.

"Get the back doors open," Mal shouted from inside the van. He had his knife out, cutting Imogen free from the cord that bound her ankles. A pair of open handcuffs lay discarded beside him. Fast work, but Emmy wouldn't have expected anything less. Meanwhile, the cashier had come to life and had his face pressed up against the glass window of the kiosk as he tried to work out what was going on.

Butt out, nothing to see here.

Emmy strode across to the dude, smiling because this was going quite well so far.

"Hi. Do you have any Twinkies?"

"Why is there a man lying on the ground? Is he okay? Should I call an ambulance?"

"Oh, he's fine. He's just got a bad back, so he works out the kinks each time we stop."

"Like yoga?"

"Exactly like yoga. He'll do the bow pose in a minute." Yup, there it was, with a little assistance from Black. Funny how it almost looked as though he was being hog-tied. "See?"

"Y'all are travelling together?"

"We sure are. Two of our friends are getting married in Vegas, and we're all on our way there, except we got delayed by an escaped horse near Amarillo, so we're running a bit late."

"That lady looks as if she's crying."

Emmy glanced across to where Mal was lifting Imogen clear of the van, her arms tight around his neck, and although tears streamed down her cheeks, she looked okay. Thank goodness.

"Yes, she's crying with happiness. That's the bride and her husband-to-be. The Twinkies?"

"Over by the magazines."

"And can I get eight coffees?"

"Uh, okay."

Emmy flipped a fifty at him. "Keep the change."

Twenty minutes later, they were on their way. They'd topped off Seacroft's gas, and one of Blackwood's guys was behind the wheel as they drove in convoy to Las Vegas. Mal cradled Imogen in the back seat of the Explorer, and Emmy glanced at them in the mirror as she followed Black and Pale, who had Seacroft stuffed into their boot.

Fake girlfriend? Yeah, right.

Emmy fished her phone out of her pocket and tapped out a message to Luther, Blackwood's head armourer, who worked out of the Richmond office.

Emmy: New pool—Mal and Imogen. I pick next Friday.

Luther: On it. I'm calling Sunday.

"Do you need to go to the hospital?" Mal asked. "Did he hurt you?"

Imogen shook her head. "He barely touched me."

Mal's eyes narrowed as Emmy's gaze flicked between the mirror and the road. Uh-oh. "*Barely* touched you?"

"He just felt me up. He said he wanted to know whether my boobs were real."

"I'll kill him."

Down boy. Although technically, it wasn't too late for murder. They could make it look like an accident. A car crash, a trip and fall, maybe a heart attack...

"Please, I just want to go home. Where am I? I don't even know where I am. He said we were going to Las Vegas."

"And you're nearly there. The plane's waiting, and we can fly straight back to Richmond."

"What'll happen to Morton? You won't really kill him, will you?"

Mal sighed. "He'll go back to Florida."

Such a shame. Emmy had even packed a nice, shiny spade she found in Pale's garage, just in case the need to lose a body arose.

"He's c-c-crazy. He said we were getting married."

"It's over. He's not getting anywhere near you again."

"H-h-how did you find me?"

"It's a long story, but I'll always find you, babe. I'm just sorry he was able to take you in the first place."

Imogen burrowed closer to Mal, her face buried in the crook of his neck, and his arms tightened around her.

"I was so scared," she mumbled.

"I know you were, babe. I know. Just rest now, okay? I've got you."

Aw, so sweet. Mal was fucked. And who knew, maybe this insane trip to Vegas would lead to the sound of wedding bells after all?

"See?" Emmy said to him. "I told you everything would be fine."

CHAPTER 18 - IMOGEN

"YOU'RE REALLY OKAY?" Stef dragged me out of Malachi's arms and wrapped me up in her own. "Emmy called Oliver and said they'd found you, but I was still so worried..."

"I'm okay, but I'm so, so tired."

Even though I'd slept on the plane, the events of the last forty-eight hours had caught up with me. Apart from when I was drugged, I'd been awake from my arrival in Florida to the moment Malachi had plucked me out of Morton's van in the middle of nowhere. And Morton had been totally insane. At first, he thought I was Misty, and when he realised I wasn't, he studied me like a laboratory specimen and told me that even though my boobs weren't so big, I was prettier so he'd marry me instead. Yes, *marry* me. The freak actually thought I'd walk down the aisle with him. He'd brought a dress and flowers and everything.

"The spare room's ready and waiting. Bridget's left food if you want any."

"I wouldn't mind something to eat."

Although I still felt sick from the shock and whatever Morton had injected me with, the nausea battled with an aching hunger. He'd kidnapped me before the wedding buffet, the asshole. Emmy had offered to stop by a fast-food joint on the way to the airport in Las Vegas, but I couldn't stomach that at the time, and now I was starving.

Malachi shifted from foot to foot in Oliver and Stef's pristine hallway. White walls, white tiles on the floor, white furniture. The only splash of colour came from the abstract paintings on the walls. Originals, of course.

"Is there anything else I can do?"

"No, really, you've done everything. The way you found me... I was terrified Morton would force me to get married. He had a gun."

"If I hadn't taken you to Florida..."

"Then it would've been Misty instead. You weren't to know there was a lunatic in the house. Well, apart from Erin."

"I'm so sorry for everything she said."

"Like you said, it's over now. Can we just forget about it?"

He stared at me for a long beat before nodding. "Sure."

Malachi wouldn't forget about it. Guilt clouded his eyes, and I wanted to explain that the only way I could deal with the horrible parts of life was to stuff them into the back of my mind and force them to stay there. If I kept talking about them, it gave me nightmares. I'd found that out when I tried visiting a therapist after what my brother did. All it led to was sleepless nights as the loosened memories replayed over and over and over.

But I was so tired that the words wouldn't come, and I yawned instead.

"I'm not even sure I'll be able to stay awake for food. I think I'll just go to bed instead."

"Then I'll see you tomorrow. Uh, the police'll want to talk to you. We can keep them away tonight, but..."

Oliver nodded. "Give them my number. I'll deal with them."

"What day is it?" I asked. "Tuesday? Aren't you supposed to be going on vacation tomorrow?"

"Not until the afternoon. They'll have to do the interview in the morning."

"Or we could postpone the trip?" Stef suggested, although Oliver didn't look particularly enamoured with that idea. "You're more important than two weeks at the beach."

"No way. You need a break, and it'll be Abby's first time abroad."

"Do you want to stay here while we're away? Bridget'll be on vacation too, but Gianni can send up food from the restaurant downstairs."

"Honestly, I'll be fine. I've got a roommate, so I won't be on my own."

And somehow, being lonely in my tiny apartment was better than rattling around in this sterile palace. It was a beautiful home, don't get me wrong—I just preferred something cosier.

"I'll be around," Malachi said. "You can call me if you need company."

That was the guilt talking, wasn't it? He had far better things to do than babysit me. But I nodded because it was easier than arguing. All I wanted to do was crawl under the perfectly pressed quilt waiting for me along the hallway.

"I will. And thanks again for everything." I managed to muster up a smile. "A proper Blackwood rescue—I guess I'm part of some sort of club now."

Even though I'd slept for fifteen hours straight, I was still exhausted. Drained. The police interrogation didn't help. Oliver sat with me the whole time and interrupted when they got too pushy, but although I explained that I couldn't remember everything, they still kept asking the same questions again and again and again. And then, because I'd been unconscious for part of the time, they insisted I go to the hospital for an examination "just in case." Having a nurse poking around down there left me feeling violated all over again.

But it was done.

And now I was on my way home, hoping Svetlana hadn't stunk the entire apartment out with incense sticks in my absence or rearranged the living room to better accommodate her yoga mat again.

Oliver drummed his fingers on the steering wheel as he waited for a traffic light to turn green. Stef was back at their apartment getting Abby ready to go, and they were in danger of missing their flight because Oliver was his usual stubborn self and refused to let me get a cab home. Roxy had offered to pick me up, but her shift in the neurosurgery ward didn't end for another three hours. I'd have been happy to wait, but Oliver insisted on doing things his way. As usual.

"You don't need to walk me up," I said as he abandoned his SUV at the kerb and jogged around to open my door. "You've done plenty already."

"Yes, I do."

There was no point in arguing; I knew that from experience. And secretly, I didn't mind Oliver's pigheadedness today because I was still jumpy. Once I'd opened the apartment door, he pecked me on the cheek and ran, and I was alone again. No Svetlana. I didn't particularly like her—we had absolutely nothing in common—but I'd still hoped she'd be home.

Then I saw the envelope on the coffee table with my name written in slanted script.

My first thought was *he's found me*, and *he* could've been Morton or Kyle or even Drew from the gym. It was just a visceral panic that made my chest seize. Then I realised the handwriting was Svetlana's and began to breathe again. Why had she left me a letter? I tore the envelope open, and a bunch of fifty-dollar bills and a note fell out.

Imogen,

Sorry for the little notice, but I meet a man last week and he ask me to travel in South America with him. We leave straight away. Life is an adventure, da? I put a month's rent for you.

Sveta xx

I didn't know what to be more upset about—that I was on my own again, or that my weird Russian lodger had managed to find a man with seemingly no effort at all.

Okay, I could do this. I could cope. The door was locked, and the landlord had fitted a new door chain for me, miracle of miracles. I'd sent him a text from the airport while I was trying to distract myself from staring at Malachi's ass, promising a six-pack of beer if he'd help me out. Guess I had to pay up now. *Breathe, Imogen.* The windows were shut tight. All I had to do was make myself dinner, watch a movie, then go to sleep. Easy.

Except it didn't quite work out that way. Every bump, every creak left me wide-eyed, and at two a.m., I tried to pile furniture against the door then burst into tears when I couldn't move the sofa.

What was wrong with me? Logically, I knew there wasn't anyone there. Kyle hadn't contacted me for years, and Seacroft was in jail. Wasn't he? What if they'd let him out on bail? Kyle skipped bail, didn't he? Then threatened to hunt me down and kill me if I pushed ahead with the court case.

By four o'clock in the morning, I couldn't stand the uncertainty any longer. Malachi did say it was okay to call, didn't he? I'd leave him a voicemail, and he could phone me back when he woke up.

"Imogen?"

"I thought you'd be asleep."

"I was."

"Sorry. I, uh, I..."

"Is something wrong?"

"No. I mean, not really. I'm on my own, and I keep hearing noises, and I just wanted to check Morton was still locked up."

"Yeah, he's still locked up. What do you mean, you're on your own? I thought you had a roommate?"

"She unexpectedly moved to South America."

Dammit, Imogen. Stop sniffling.

"I'm on my way over."

What? "No! It's late. Early. I'm fine, really, just being stupid."

"I'll call when I'm coming up the stairs."

Shit. What had I done?

CHAPTER 19 - IMOGEN

"I DIDN'T MEAN for you to come over."

Malachi dumped a duffel bag in the living room and surveyed the haphazard furniture. I'd tried to put it back, but the adrenaline that helped me to move it in the first place had seeped away.

"I know."

"You don't have to stay."

"I'll sleep on the sofa."

"I'm not sure you'll fit on the sofa."

It was only a two-seater, and Malachi was at least six feet tall and built of muscles.

"Then I'll borrow your ex-roommate's bed."

"She didn't have a bed. There was one when she moved in, but she sold it on Craigslist one day while I was out at work."

Yet another reason we hadn't seen eye to eye. She thought that since she gave me the fifty bucks, it was okay, but now I had to find a new bed for my next roommate. I blinked back the tears that threatened to escape. Buying a bed might not sound like much, but on top of everything else, it was another burden I didn't want to shoulder. I was in danger of breaking, perhaps as close as I'd ever been.

"Craigslist?" Malachi shook his head and unzipped his bag. "What did she sleep on?"

"A yoga mat sprinkled with rose petals. And she used to put crystals under her pillow."

The organic cotton pillow that she'd gotten delivered from a cooperative based just outside Kathmandu. I always thought it smelled funky, probably because it was stuffed with yak hair.

Malachi opened the door to her room, and sure enough, the rose petals were still there, shrivelled and stuck to the carpet along with half a ton of ash from her incense and a package of spirulina powder she'd spilled and never bothered to clear up. She hated vacuum cleaners. Said the noise unbalanced her chakras.

"Stinks in there."

"I know."

"I'll sleep on the floor in the living room." Before I could argue, he held up a hand. "I've slept in worse places, believe me. Just go back to bed, babe. Nice pyjamas, by the way."

I hadn't even thought about what I was wearing, but now I glanced down and saw my traitorous nipples poking through the pink silk. Malachi had that effect on me, even when my mind was on other things. My cheeks heated, and I backed hastily towards my bedroom.

Slam.

I leaned against the door, breathing hard. Perhaps I should buy new sleepwear? Everything I owned was on the, uh, risqué side. Take tonight's pyjamas, for example—the shorts barely covered my ass, and with a certain Blackwood employee around, that could be a problem. I was like Pavlov's dog with Malachi's freaking pheromones. Why had I called him? *Stupid, stupid Imogen.* Tomorrow night, I'd do the sensible thing and take a sleeping pill.

"What on earth are you doing?" I asked as I stumbled out of my bedroom on Thursday morning. I'd expected Malachi to be long gone, but instead, he was on his knees in the spare room, brushing the worst of Svetlana's mess into a dustpan.

"Cleaning up."

"Aren't you supposed to be at work?"

"My hours are flexible." He nodded towards the living room, where his laptop was open on the coffee table. "I can catch up on paperwork from here. What about you? Do you have to work today?"

"I don't know yet. I need to call Lisa." She, Charlene, and Stef had held the fort while I'd been away, working extra hours and rearranging appointments. I'd spoken with her briefly to let her know I was home, and she assured me everything was under control if I needed some time off. But I preferred to be back at work. The salon was a sanctuary, and I'd have company there. "I'll probably go in this afternoon."

"I'll drive you. The coffee machine's on, or I can go out and pick up breakfast if you want."

"You don't need to do all this."

"I know I don't need to, but I want to."

If Malachi didn't stop being so nice, it was me who'd be feeling guilty, not him.

"Imogen!" Jean-Luc held his arms open, a paper carrier bag in one outstretched hand. "I heard you had a terrible accident?"

I let him gather me up and sighed as I found my happy place. Well, one of them. When Malachi kissed me softly on the cheek outside the salon at lunchtime, I'd felt pretty damn happy as well.

"It wasn't an accident," I mumbled into Jean-Luc's shoulder. "I got kidnapped."

"Mon Dieu! But you escaped?"

"Sort of. I got rescued."

"Thank goodness for the police. Here, I brought you mille-feuille with double chocolate icing. I know it's your favourite."

Oh, Jean-Luc. That was him all over—whenever I got down, he tried to cheer me up. While I was stuck on a grimy mattress in the back of Morton's van with my hands and feet cuffed and bound and duct-taped together, I'd tried to distract myself by imagining my favourite indulgences. Jean-Luc's pastries had been high on the list, behind the man himself and...Malachi.

Okay, I confess, I'd thought about Malachi more than I should have while I was trapped. A bad case of wanting what I couldn't have? What I *shouldn't* have? Jean-Luc was my dream man, so why, for the last week, had Malachi come to me every night while I slept?

Jean-Luc ticked all my boxes—kind, straightforward, easy on the eye. Jean-Luc was frothy cocoa on a cold winter's evening. Malachi was fire. Unpredictable, deadly, and liable to burn me if I handled him wrong. The hot ones were always dangerous to a girl's heart.

I took the bag of pastries. "You're too sweet."

"I thought we could eat them over coffee. Or dinner?"

Dinner? "Don't you have to work tonight?"

"I have the evening off, and I hate to see you sad."

Dinner. Malachi was meant to be picking me up from the salon, but I couldn't turn down Jean-Luc. I sent a quick text saying I was safe and that I'd be back later, because I didn't want another Blackwood search party out looking for me, then I took Jean-Luc's arm as we headed three blocks over to a little Japanese restaurant that had just opened.

"Checking out the competition?" I asked, trying to smile.

"Call it professional curiosity. Gaston's thinking of running a Japanese week at Rhodium. A friend of his is a chef in Tokyo, and they might do a kitchen swap."

"Wouldn't that be tricky? A temporary chef wouldn't know where anything was."

"He doesn't speak much English either, but the publicity would be worth the logistical headaches. It'd be busy—would you want to work a few shifts?"

Go back to waitressing? No, thank you, not right now. I didn't miss it. "The salon's doing well at the moment."

"*C'est fantastique.* Do you have a lot to catch up on?"

I shook my head. "The others shuffled things around and worked extra hours."

"Good staff are hard to find." He reached across the table and squeezed my hand. "We miss you at Rhodium."

Once, that touch would have made me shiver, but tonight, I was numb to Jean-Luc's charms. A warped reaction to the shock of being kidnapped? Or had spending too much time around Malachi ruined me?

I still hadn't figured out the answer by the time our appetisers arrived. Pork gyoza for Jean-Luc—little fried dumplings—and tempura for me. Slightly soggy, Jean-Luc said, and I couldn't imagine him making the same mistake. Still, I ate everything, grateful that my appetite had finally made a reappearance.

"So," Jean-Luc said, leaning his elbows on the table after the waiter cleared our dishes away. "What happened? In Florida, I mean. Lisa wasn't sure of the details. Do you know you made the news?"

Hear that flapping sound? That was my appetite flying out the door.

"I did?"

"The police put out an appeal for anyone that saw you or some van. Is that what you got kidnapped in?"

I managed to nod.

"Mon Dieu. I've never met anyone who genuinely got kidnapped before. At least, I don't think so. Back when I was a teenager, I bussed tables at a restaurant in Paris, and the sous chef there swore he once got abducted by aliens."

"It definitely wasn't aliens who took me."

"Did you know the guy well? I mean, did he ever look at you oddly?"

"I'd never met him before. Maybe we could talk about something else?"

"*Je suis desolé.* Of course. How was the wedding until that point?"

Not much better. I still had Erin's claw marks decorating my back, red lines and scabby bits where she'd caught my skin with her nails. Lisa had redone mine today, fixing the broken one while I tried not to cry. For years, I'd plastered on a cheerful face, always the party girl, but every day, it got more difficult.

"The bride was friendly, and...and...the drinks table was well-stocked."

"That reminds me, one of the reps brought in some excellent wine samples. I'll bring a bottle over tomorrow for you to try. Imogen, I heard rumours the kidnapper was pretending to be a waiter—is that true?"

"I think he really *did* work for the catering company at one point."

And so it went on. Jean-Luc's curiosity was only natural, I guess, but I still couldn't stomach my main course. Then Marelaine texted, and he gave me an apologetic smile.

"I'm afraid I'm being summoned. Perhaps we could take dessert with us?"

That actually sounded like a good idea. "Sure."

"Sorry."

"Honestly, it's okay."

I just wanted to get home before I cried. Talking about my ordeal had left me shaking inside. And as I jogged from Jean-Luc's Peugeot into my building, I realised something. In all his questions—his whole interrogation, for want of a better word—he'd never once asked if I was okay.

That revelation made me choke as I scurried up the stairs. *Don't cry on the landing, Imogen.* And why wouldn't my key fit in the lock? I tried once, twice, three times, and it refused to go in.

A shadow moved across the peephole in the door. "Imogen?"

Wait. I didn't have a freaking peephole.

The door swung open, and I clutched at my chest as Malachi tucked the gun back into his waistband.

"How did you get home?" he asked. "I said I'd pick you up."

"You nearly gave me a heart attack!"

"Sorry." At least he had the good grace to look contrite. "How did you get home?" he asked again.

"Jean-Luc brought me."

Malachi stepped forward and peered along the hallway. "Where is he?"

"Downstairs. He didn't come in."

"Asshole," Malachi muttered under his breath. "Are you okay? You don't look okay."

Now the tears came. I couldn't hold them back any longer. Crying in front of Malachi was perhaps the worst part of my entire week. During my rescue, it had been sort of understandable—I mean, I was allowed to be emotional at that point—but now?

"I-I-I'm fine."

He wrapped his arms around me, and it turned out that as well as being a superhero stuffed into the body of a fitness model, Malachi gave really good hugs. I fell a little bit more in love with him at that point—stupid, pointless love, but love nonetheless. At least, until I wiped my tears away and realised he'd turned my living room into a building site.

"Why is there a door on my couch?"

Hadn't I just walked through the front door? I turned to check, and sure enough...two doors.

"I installed a new one."

"Why?"

"Because your old one was shit. Flimsy as hell. This one's steel-reinforced with a bump-proof five-point locking system."

"I don't understand any of what you just said."

"It's more difficult to break through."

"My landlord..."

"Should've fitted a better door."

"What if I lose my key?"

"I'll leave a spare at Blackwood. Just call the control room, and someone'll bring it over."

He made it all sound so simple. "But...but I can't afford a new door right now."

Not when Svetlana had left and I needed to hunt for yet another new roommate.

"Nothing for you to pay. Since you're on the fourth floor and you don't have a balcony, window bars aren't a strict necessity but an alarm is. My go-to guy isn't around until next Thursday, though."

"An alarm? You don't have to do all this."

He gave me a sweet but sheepish smile. "I just want you to be safe."

"I think I need wine."

I wriggled out of his arms because otherwise I might have been tempted to do something totally dumb like kiss him. Stef had left an emergency bottle of rosé in the fridge, and tonight definitely qualified. But when I yanked the fridge door open, the wine was hidden away behind a ton of food I didn't recall buying. Kale? Carrots? Lean ground beef? No, that definitely wasn't mine. I was more of a TV dinners kind of a girl.

"What's all this stuff?"

"I thought I'd cook, but..." He nodded towards my doggy bag, which was literally shaped like a dog. Some sort of small terrier, if I wasn't mistaken. "It looks as though you've already eaten."

Malachi had planned to make us dinner? My ovaries clambered up my throat and slapped me for not getting home earlier.

"I'm so sorry, I..."

"It'll keep till tomorrow. I'll clear up here, then we can go to bed. I had one of those delivered too—hope you don't mind."

Mind? I was tempted to climb into it with him. "That's okay. Thank you."

He leaned past me and rummaged around in the fridge. "Here's that wine. Pour me a glass too, would you?"

I should have bought an extra bottle.

Chapter 20 - Malachi

WHAT WAS THAT awful noise? Mal woke to the sound of muffled country music shaking the ceiling above his head. Fuck, it was six a.m. Where was his gun?

He stumbled out of the bedroom in his boxers and almost ran into a sleepy-eyed Imogen. She hadn't gotten dressed either, and Mal's cock twitched at the sight of her in a scrap of pale pink silk that barely covered any part of her.

"You're not going out like that."

"What? Of course I'm not going out like this. I'm going to make coffee."

"You're not planning to complain about the noise?"

"The music? No, it's pointless. The guy upstairs plays it every morning at the same time, Friday through Tuesday, and he refuses to turn it down. Wednesday and Thursday seem to be his days off, and he likes to sleep in. On those days, we get a reprieve until noon. The landlord doesn't care."

"I care. Want me to have a word with him?"

"He's scary. Besides, it means I don't have to remember to set the alarm."

Nobody was as scary as Emmy before coffee. A rowdy neighbour would be a walk in the park. Mal retreated to the spare bedroom to pull on a pair of pants then flashed a grin at Imogen.

"Make the coffee, babe. I'll be back in five."

Her mouth opened. Closed. Opened again, and he could tell she was ready to argue, so he quickly slipped out of the door. What kind of asshole deafened his neighbours on five mornings out of seven? Mal was about to find out.

Or was he?

It wasn't difficult to identify the source of the noise —the door was vibrating. But over the din, Mal heard the faint sound of running water and somebody singing along. The asshole was in the shower?

Mal had his wallet in his pants pocket, and he extracted the set of lock picks that sat behind his bank cards. A minute later, the door swung open, and sure enough, steam rolled out of the bathroom door. Mal could just about make out the flabby figure wedged into the shower cubicle, tugging at his privates. A wanker in more ways than one, as Emmy would say.

The stereo, complete with a pair of giant speakers, sat on a low table next to the bedroom window, right above where Imogen slept on the floor below. Mal opened the window, checked there was nobody walking below, and tossed the offending items out. Problem solved. He'd left before the asshole even got out of the bathroom.

Downstairs, Imogen was pacing the living room, and she still hadn't gotten dressed.

"There, problem solved."

"What did you do? You didn't hurt him, did you?"

Mal shook his head and steered her through to the bedroom. When he opened the window and motioned to the mess of scattered electronics below, the small crowd that had gathered looked up and applauded.

"That. Let me know if he gets another one."

"Didn't he try to stop you?"

"He was busy in the bathroom."

"Busy? Like, pooping?"

"Nah, babe. *Busy.*"

She stared at him for a beat then burst out laughing. Proper belly laughs, holding her stomach, and fuck was that good to see.

"Ohmigosh! He was jerking off to Earl Thomas Conley?"

"You know who that is?"

"Sure I do. I'm from... Never mind."

She clammed up, suddenly serious again.

"From where, babe?"

A hesitation. Why didn't she want to talk about her origins?

"From Portsmouth, Ohio." When she finally spoke, it came out as a whisper. "At least, I was born there, same as Earl Thomas Conley. My family moved to Cleveland when I was six."

"Your family..." Ah, dammit, Mal was gonna go to hell for this. "When I first told Stefanie you were missing, she mentioned a problem with your brother. She thought he might have taken you."

The effect was instantaneous. Imogen turned white, stiffened, and backed away. When she realised the wall was behind her, and she had nowhere to go, she sucked in a mouthful of air. And another. Then another.

"What's wrong?"

"Nothing."

"Bullshit."

"Just don't talk about my brother, o-o-okay?"

Was this a panic attack? Was Imogen having a

panic attack? Mal slid an arm around her waist and guided her over to the sofa.

"Okay. But whatever he did to you... Right now, I'm tempted to pay him a visit, and I don't mean just to throw his stereo out the window."

"Y-y-you won't find him. The police couldn't find him."

The cops were involved? In Cleveland? If Mal bumped this up the priority list, Mack could dig up everything there was to know if she had a name to go on... What was Imogen's surname? Blair? Yes, Blair. He'd seen it on her mail yesterday.

"If you want me to find him, I'll find him."

She stared at the wall for a long while, glassy-eyed. Did she need a doctor? Mal got up to turn off the heat when the kettle started whistling, and she still hadn't moved when he got back. He squeezed her hand, and she clung on in a vice-like grip.

Finally, she spoke in a deathly whisper. "It's better to move on. I've moved on."

"No, you haven't. Not if he still terrifies you this way."

"I'm getting better. Ten years... It's halfway now."

"Halfway? What's halfway?"

Mal had to lean closer to hear her reply.

"The statute of limitations."

If halfway was ten years, then what had a twenty-year statute of limitations in Ohio? Legal talk got bandied around the office all the time, and Mal racked his brain. Fuck. Oh fuck, oh fuck, oh fuck. Tell him he was wrong.

"Imogen, did your brother rape you?"

This morning's tears were worse than last night's,

and all Mal could do was hug her as she wept the pain out. And there was a lot of pain. Mal had his answer, even if it was one he didn't want to hear.

"He can't get to you now; I promise."

"At first when I w-w-was in the back of the van, I thought it was Kyle driving, then Morton spoke, and I realised it wasn't, and I was relieved. Is that crazy? I was relieved because I'd gotten kidnapped by a regular freak instead of my brother."

Kyle. Kyle Blair. Mal filed the name away. "It's not crazy at all. You were seventeen when he attacked you?"

"The last time, yes. Seventeen."

Every word out of her mouth made things worse. "The last time? He did it more than once?"

"The first time, he was fourteen, and I was eleven. And I thought it was freaking normal! He told me it was, and I didn't know any better until I got older. Then it was too late. He wouldn't stop."

"Did you tell your parents?"

"My mom? Not then. She worshipped Kyle."

"Your father?"

"He's serving life in prison for armed robbery. Mom thinks *he's* innocent too."

"And you don't?"

"No way. He was always violent, even before that."

Mal squeezed Imogen tighter, and she squashed against his side, knees drawn up to her chest. Imogen was broken. The last week had destroyed her, and he didn't know whether to keep probing or let her shut down. Emmy always said it helped her to talk about the shit she dealt with, that sharing allowed her to sleep at night, although she only confided in her husband. Mal decided to push on, gently.

"But you told the police?"

"I didn't want to. But the d-d-doctor, she convinced me."

"The doctor? What doctor? Did Kyle put you in the hospital?"

"Sort of." Now she was back to the glassy-eyed stare. "He got me pregnant."

Holy shit. "What happened to the baby?"

Imogen's shoulders shook as if she wanted to cry but she'd run out of tears. Mal felt like a shit for ever starting this conversation. Why hadn't he just bought a pair of earplugs?

"I told Kyle what he'd done. I guess I thought maybe he'd leave me alone for a while, but he punched me in the stomach instead. By the time I got to the doctor's, I was already miscarrying. And the doctor said I should tell the police, that there was evidence now."

The foetus. DNA. Kyle Blair was a dead man. It took all Mal's willpower to keep his ass on the sofa rather than driving straight to Blackwood HQ and raiding the weapons locker. One bullet to the brain was all it would take.

"The police brought charges?"

"They came to interview me, but Mom told them I was a troublemaker. Always seeking attention, those were her words. The police officers were real kind, and they said they'd bring Kyle in, but Mom warned him they were coming so he kept clear of the house. That was when he threatened to kill me. One day on the way home from school, he forced me into an empty building and held a knife against my throat. Said if I went ahead and pressed charges, he'd cut clean through to my spine. I can still hear him now, whispering with his breath on my ear."

"You're safe here. Nobody's coming through that door."

"I'll never be safe. He hates me, and he never lets go of a grudge."

"Why? Did you press charges?"

"I tried to, but the police still couldn't find him. By that time, I'd left home. It was summer, and I found a job picking apples on a farm outside the city. The farmer and his wife were real sweet, and they let me sleep in an old trailer behind the barn, but I hadn't gone far enough. Kyle found me there. I didn't sleep so well, and I heard him at the door one night, trying to get in."

No wonder she was jumpy about doors. "You're sure it was him?"

"Yes. I climbed out the window, and when he got into my bedroom and turned the light on, I saw him. That was the night I travelled to Richmond. Just rode the bus without even knowing where I was going, and this was where I ended up."

"But you've done well for yourself. Didn't you go to university?"

Mal may have asked Oliver a few questions about Imogen after he first met her. Nothing that would arouse too many suspicions, but he'd gotten curious. Except now she buried her head in her hands.

"I lied. I've lied to too many people, people I care about."

"You *didn't* go to university?"

"Not properly. I hung around on campus and snuck into classes because I felt safe there, but I was never enrolled. Hell, I didn't even finish high school."

Which was a true tragedy because Imogen was smart. Damn smart, and brave too.

"And I bet you're wondering how I ended up as an escort, aren't you? Especially with my history."

"You did what you had to. You're a survivor, babe."

"I needed the money—that was part of it. But I wanted... I wanted two things, really. Firstly, I'd watched too many movies and I dreamed of meeting a man who'd rescue me, and secondly, I wanted to have sex on my terms, like my own kind of therapy. Sometimes, men would pay extra for a girl to hurt them, and I fucking enjoyed it."

Ouch. Mal's testicles shrivelled at her tone, but she was still holding his hand, which had to count for something, right? He gave a little squeeze, both as a reminder that he was there for her and as an apology for all mankind.

"I guess I can't blame you for that."

"For a while, I got off on the control, and it also meant I could afford to live. But then I began to hate myself for liking it. Does that sound weird?"

Yes. "As I said, you did what you had to."

"And I realised I'd never have a chance at happiness if I kept working for Rubies. So I quit. And I thought if I acted like the kind of girl I wanted to be—you know, happy and fun-loving—maybe one day it'd become real. But it's getting harder and harder to pretend."

"Then stop. Stop pretending."

"How can I? I see my friends settling down with amazing guys, and I want that too. But what man would deal with my baggage?"

"I thought you wanted Jean-Luc?"

Imogen chewed on her bottom lip.

"Yes. Yes, I do. But he only knows some of my past, not all of it." She gave Mal a tiny smile. "You're the only person who knows all of it. Jean-Luc would run a mile if I unloaded on him like that. I'm surprised you haven't."

Honestly, so was Mal. But there was something about Imogen that drew him in. Beautiful but broken. Cute but with claws. Sweet, but now he knew she had an edge. She knew his past, and she hadn't held it against him, so now he had to grant her the same understanding.

"I'll always be here if you need someone to talk to. Friends?"

Her smile widened infinitesimally. "Friends."

"You're a helluva strong woman, Imogen Blair."

"Imogen Thomas," she mumbled. "Blair's my middle name. I dropped my surname when I had to hide."

Imogen Blair Thomas.

I, Malachi Steven Banks take this woman, Imogen Blair Thomas... Whoa! What the fuck? Had he lost his damn mind?

Focus, man.

Focus.

Kyle Thomas was a dead man.

CHAPTER 21 - IMOGEN

WHAT WAS IT called when you went temporarily insane? Was there a technical term for it? Because I'd certainly lost my mind. Why had I just told possibly the hottest and also the kindest man I'd ever met about my dark past?

A blip in my consciousness? A delayed reaction to my abduction? Or was it a defence mechanism? Was I trying to scare Malachi off before I fell completely in love with him? I'd never been stupid enough to spill my guts to Jean-Luc like that. What was wrong with me?

"Don't you have to work?" I asked Malachi on Friday morning.

"Not until later. I've got a hostage rescue drill this afternoon, but I'm not sure what time. How about you? Do you have to go to the salon?"

"Lisa told me I should take some time off, so she moved all my appointments over to her and Charlene. I was gonna head in anyway, but now I think I might go back to bed instead."

And if I drank the bottle of Unisom from the bathroom cabinet, I might actually fall asleep instead of reliving my mistakes over and over and over again.

"You're tired?"

"Tired of life? Very much so."

Malachi's phone vibrated, and he glanced at the

screen.

"Good news. Emmy's rescheduled the training drill, so I can take the day off. What do you want to do? Go out for lunch? Watch a movie?"

"With you?"

"That was the general idea."

"After everything I said last night, you want to spend time with me?"

"Sure."

He felt sorry for me, didn't he? That was why. Well, I didn't need his pity.

"Thanks for the offer, but I'll be okay on my own."

His answer? He got up, walked over to the kitchen cupboard—*my* kitchen cupboard—pulled out a package of popcorn, and put it in the microwave.

"Guess I'll have to eat this on my own."

"What?"

He dropped back onto the sofa and fished the remote out of its spot down the side of the cushion.

"Can't beat Netflix and chill for a day off."

"I don't have Netflix."

"Yeah, you do. I installed it on your TV last night."

"So you plan to sit in my living room all day, eating popcorn and watching movies?"

"Yup." He dropped his voice to a whisper. "But don't worry, I'll keep the volume down if you want to sleep."

"You're impossible."

"There's plenty of popcorn for two. Don't say I didn't offer."

Dammit. Yes, it was my apartment, and I could have pushed him to leave—and I had no doubts he would have—but this was Malachi, so I couldn't bring myself to kick him out. I liked him, okay? Perhaps even more than I liked popcorn.

"Fine. But no horror movies. The last thing I want to see this week is a dismembered corpse."

"Deal. You can pick whatever you want."

CHAPTER 22 - MALACHI

ON SATURDAY MORNING, Mal's back was still cricked from Friday's movie marathon. Imogen had fallen asleep on him—literally on him, since she'd keeled over and landed in his lap—and he hadn't moved a muscle through the whole of the third Bridget Jones movie. They'd watched the first two already, then Imogen had woken up and insisted on watching the one she'd slept through again from the beginning, and Mal didn't even care because he liked having her close. Thank goodness she'd put on a T-shirt and a pair of sweatpants or he'd have been in trouble.

But now she meandered into the blessedly silent kitchen in another one of those tiny nighties, and he stifled a groan.

"Do you always wear those things at night?"

"I like them. They remind me of the old black-and-white movies Stef's always watching. Why? What's wrong with it?"

"Nothing. Just curious. Here, I made coffee."

Not the instant she usually drank. Mal had unearthed a French press from the back of a cupboard and made filter coffee with the grounds he'd brought with him. Emmy was a bad influence—she insisted on having good coffee in the Blackwood offices at all times, and now Mal couldn't stand anything else.

He'd jogged to the café along the street and picked up danishes too. Cinnamon for him, plus one apricot and a chocolate chip for Imogen. Her sweet tooth hadn't escaped his notice. It was probably why she had her heart set on dating a fucking pastry chef. Mal could cook the basics, but he'd never be able to master the twiddly desserts.

"It's a shame you're not looking for a place to live," she said. "I could use a new roommate."

Mal was tempted. He was actually tempted. The rent would be nothing—Blackwood paid him very well —but he couldn't stand the thought of watching her gallivanting around with Monsieur Francais.

"You'll find someone, babe. Who wouldn't want to live with you?"

"I always seem to attract the weirdos, and it's a bonus if they actually pay the rent."

"Let me know when you have a candidate, and I'll get the background check done through Blackwood."

"Really?"

Her face lit up. Imogen was easily pleased by the small things, and he hated that something so mundane as a background check could be the highlight of her day.

"No problem. Are you working today?"

"Just this morning. You?"

"I have a meeting this morning, and I need to fit in a quick gym session this afternoon. Other than that, I'm all yours."

"Which gym do you use?"

"Blackwood's."

"Oh."

"Why?"

"I probably should start going to the gym. I thought that last week, but then Drew happened, and I cancelled the membership I never used anyway."

"Blackwood's headquarters is a trek if you don't drive, but the Richmond office has a small gym in the basement. I'll get you a pass."

"They won't mind?"

"I wouldn't have offered otherwise. Do you want to go today? Or do you have other plans?"

Imogen's lips scrunched to the side as if she was trying to make up her mind. "I was supposed to go out clubbing with some people I used to work with this evening, but I don't really want to. No more pretending, right?"

"No more pretending, Miss Thomas."

For a moment, she stiffened, and Mal saw the effort it took her to relax and smile. Baby steps.

"Shall I meet you at Blackwood's office? I know where it is."

"I'll pick you up from the salon instead. About one o'clock?"

"I think I'm looking forward to it."

"Well?" Emmy stopped in front of Mal, hands on hips, studying his face. "Dammit."

"Am I missing something?"

"Clearly. You're smiling, but it's not the smile of a man who got laid last night."

"What the hell are you talking about?" Then it dawned on him. "Are you running a pool on me and Imogen?"

"Of course we are."

"Is that why you postponed yesterday's training session?"

"It might have been."

"You do realise we're only pretending to date? She's got her heart set on some fucker who cooks meringues for a living."

"Yeah, but that won't work out. Beyond the cakes, there's not an awful lot of substance to Jean-Luc."

"You think?"

"I spoke to Oliver about him. The dude has a new woman every six weeks. It's like he gets bored quickly. If you don't man up and make a move before she finds out he's just a dick with an oven, you'd better make sure you're around to pick up the pieces."

Shit. Tomorrow was the big day, their "date" to the cooking contest. And while Mal would definitely be around to pick up the pieces if it came to that, he didn't want Imogen to get her heart broken again. She'd been through enough already.

That meant he'd have to say something tonight. But where did he start?

"Earth to Mal. Meeting's starting in ten. D'ya want coffee?"

"Yeah, and I also want to talk to you. I need to find a guy."

"A guy? What guy?"

"His name's Kyle Thomas. Ten years ago, he raped a woman in Cleveland and skipped town before he could be charged."

Emmy sucked in a deep breath. "Does this have something to do with Imogen?"

"Yes."

"Fuck. I always thought there was a hint of sadness under all those smiles, but I hoped I was wrong."

"She's tough."

"Yeah, she is. We'll find Kyle Thomas. Give Mack everything you know, and we'll start looking. Oh, I do have one small piece of good news—we tracked down the pig Imogen met in the gym."

That *was* good news. "Where does he live? I'll have a word."

"No need. Me and Fia already paid him a visit."

Oh, fuck. "What did you do to him?"

Emmy patted Mal on the arm and flashed him a worryingly chipper grin.

"You probably don't want to know."

Imogen was chatting to a brunette—a client by the look of her fancy manicure—when Malachi arrived at Nailed It. He took a seat on the grey leather sofa by the door to wait, but he couldn't help overhearing some of their conversation.

"Aw, it's a shame you don't feel like coming out tonight, but we're probably gonna go to a restaurant for Becky's birthday instead of the club."

"Really? But she loves clubbing."

"We all do, but some of the boys don't want to go. A guy my brother knows from the gym went out drinking last night, met a girl, and woke up in bed this morning with a sheep tattooed on his forehead. He's got no idea how it got there, and the others are a bit wary of it happening to them."

"How can somebody not remember getting

tattooed?"

The brunette shrugged. "No idea, but that's what I heard. Can you book me in for three weeks' time? I need infills, and I'm thinking of some of those little diamonds."

"Sure. Saturday again?"

A tattoo? Mal only knew two women crazy enough to pull that stunt, and if it was true, he owed both of them a drink.

He fired off a message to Emmy.

Mal: A sheep? Really?

Emmy: It was supposed to be a pig, but Sofia jogged my arm and it went a bit wonky.

She sent a picture too, and it looked like the result of a genetic experiment gone wrong. Was that a fifth leg or an oversized penis?

Mal: You need to work on your drawing skills.

Emmy: Bite me.

He could only chuckle as Imogen picked up her purse. Emmy might be notoriously headstrong and difficult to work with at times, but she always had her people's backs. And with Drew's payback ticked off the list, Mal had a more pressing problem at hand—how to convince Imogen to buy American.

In the gym, he kept getting distracted—partly by people stopping to talk because he rarely visited the Richmond office, but mostly because Imogen wore an outfit that showed every fucking curve, and she had a lot of those. It didn't escape his notice how many of the other men stared at her too, and he had to attack the weight pile so he didn't knock somebody's teeth out.

He'd speak to her after dinner. On the way back to her place, they stopped at Claude's Patisserie and picked up *gâteau opéra* for dessert, because surely that had to be a point in his favour, and he'd already bought the ingredients for ravioli with buttered lemon greens. Okay, so he'd cheated and got the ravioli from the Italian deli, and the dish wasn't as fancy as anything the damn chef would come up with, but it was simple enough that Mal wouldn't screw it up when he got distracted by Imogen's ass.

And she seemed to appreciate his efforts. She liked to eat well rather than picking at her food, and that was yet another thing Mal loved about her. Loved? Really? Fuck, it was heading that way.

He watched her wine consumption carefully, waiting for that optimum moment where her guard was lowered but she wasn't drunk. Another half-glass, he estimated, pouring smoothly.

"Where did you learn to cook like that?" she asked.

Prison. He'd taken basic cookery classes because it was better than sitting in his cell. But he didn't want to rehash the past tonight, even though Imogen had been more understanding about his than he'd ever dared to hope a woman would be.

"Cooking Channel. I burned everything at first."

"I wish I could cook better. Jean-Luc keeps saying he'll teach me, but he's always busy."

"I'll cook with you if you want."

"You will?"

Fuck, he loved it when she smiled like that.

"Yeah, and when we mess up, I'll order us a takeout."

Imogen reached across the table and squeezed his hand, an action he felt in his heart too. Still a quarter of a glass of wine to go...

"Thank you for being here. And for everything else. If I was on my own tonight, I'd probably lose my mind."

"I'll always be here for you. I'm only ever a phone call away." And hopefully, most of the time, a hell of a lot closer. "Ready for dessert?"

"Am I ever. I've been looking forward to that all evening."

Dessert and wine. Now was the time. Except no sooner had Imogen taken the last mouthful of cake than her phone rang. Then rang again. And again. "Habanera" from *Carmen*—Mal recognised the song. He'd briefly dallied with an opera singer during a six-week work trip to Paris a couple of years back, and she'd attempted to educate him in French culture, which had been cool apart from her disconcerting habit of bursting into song in the bedroom.

Imogen gave an apologetic grimace. "I'd better get that. It's Jean-Luc."

The asshole had his own damn ring tone?

"Sure. I'll clear up."

She retreated to her room, and before she closed the door, Mal heard her talking softly to the competition. And she didn't reappear.

Mal could hardly burst into her bedroom, could he? Acting like a caveman would hardly endear him to a fragile woman he'd sworn to protect. No, he had to retreat to bed alone and lick his wounds instead, hoping for a miracle in the morning.

CHAPTER 23 - IMOGEN

OH, HELL! I'D fallen asleep.

After I'd got off the phone with Jean-Luc, I'd only meant to sit for a few minutes. I'd intended to reply to messages from Stef and Roxy and let my overheated libido cool down, but instead I woke at three in the morning with a stiff neck and a horrible feeling of guilt. When I crept into the kitchen, I found Malachi had put everything away and done the dishes, and his bedroom door was firmly closed.

Imogen, you dumbass. I hadn't even wanted to speak to Jean-Luc, but I'd needed to get out of Malachi's way before I lost my mind and kissed him. Or crawled into his lap. Or reached for his damn zipper. And Jean-Luc had only called to say his cooking slot had been moved half an hour earlier to eleven thirty. Why he hadn't just sent a text message, I had no idea.

In all honesty, the prospect of going to La Parade Des Chefs didn't appeal in the slightest anymore. I preferred eating the food to watching it being cooked, and the thought of spending another day near Marelaine filled me with dread.

So why was I still going?

Because if it meant I got one last "date" with Malachi, I'd endure any amount of cattiness and sniping and hints about free manicures.

But first, I had to apologise for leaving him with the dirty dishes last night as well as pulling a disappearing act. Which would perhaps have been easier if I could walk. I stumbled out of my bedroom like a drunk, clutching at the wall for support as my hamstrings burned and my back twinged.

"A little sore?" Malachi asked.

Of course, he looked perfectly composed, leaning against the dining table with a mug of coffee in his hand.

"How do people go to the gym every day?"

"Once your muscles build up, it doesn't hurt anymore."

"I'm not sure I'll ever be able to walk properly again. I need one of those motorised carts you get in Walmart."

"In that case, why don't you stay home today? I can pick up lunch and bring it over."

Really? Hmm... Lunch with Malachi was a whole lot more appealing than lunch with Marelaine and five hundred strangers. But then the guilt hit again, a sucker punch to the gut. Jean-Luc was a friend, and he'd saved me two tickets that he could have given to someone else if I'd cancelled in advance. I had to put in an appearance at least.

"No, no, I'll be fine. I have Advil."

Malachi didn't look particularly convinced by my declaration, but he filled me a glass with water while I dug through the bathroom cabinet. How many of these pills could I take in one go? Right now, I needed the whole damn lot.

I'll be fine. I'll be fine. I'll be fine.

I repeated the mantra over and over, but even I

wasn't entirely convinced.

Malachi had bought me breakfast again, a white-chocolate-and-raspberry muffin this time. And he made better coffee than I ever did. This was what I needed in a man. Somebody who cared. Somebody who'd be there to hold me up when I was at my lowest. And I was becoming more and more doubtful that that somebody was Jean-Luc.

Should I tell Malachi how I felt? What was the worst that could happen? That he'd run a mile and our new "friends" arrangement would be null and void? I didn't think I could stand that, not when I'd only just gotten to know him.

So I kept my mouth shut, put on a pretty dress and dainty pumps, and climbed into the Camaro beside him for the trip to Le Parade des Chefs. Yes, he had a Camaro. This was the car he'd picked me up in that horrible night a year ago, the night he'd saved me from getting arrested, and the car had a lot to answer for. It was where my stupid attraction to Malachi had started, and the vibrations from the engine weren't helping today either.

At least when we arrived, I had an excuse for holding his hand. For putting my arm around him and leaning into him when he kissed my hair. And then there was the absolutely glorious moment when Marelaine caught sight of him for the first time, and her jaw actually dropped.

My smile was genuine as I made the introductions. Even Jean-Luc looked surprised.

"Jean-Luc, Marelaine, meet Malachi. Malachi, this is Jean-Luc, one of my colleagues from Rhodium, and Marelaine, his girlfriend."

Malachi shook Jean-Luc's hand, kissed Marelaine's, then beamed at both of them. "It's good to finally meet some of Imogen's friends."

Jean-Luc swallowed. "Likewise. How long have you been dating?"

"Only a few weeks, but it feels like much longer, doesn't it, babe?"

"It does. Sometimes, the heart just knows what it wants."

"How did you meet?" Marelaine asked.

Malachi answered again. "Through a mutual friend. My lucky day. Imogen's the girl I've been waiting for my whole life."

If I hadn't known better, I might have believed Malachi meant that. He sure was a good actor. Probably it came from all that undercover work the Blackwood team did.

I stood on tiptoes to kiss him on the cheek. "*Our* lucky day."

A lady with a clipboard meandered past and pointed at Jean-Luc with her pen. "Five minutes, Monsieur Fortier."

"I'd better get my chef's whites on. There should be three seats with your names on them right at the front."

Sure enough, there they were. Marelaine Oliveira, Imogen Blair, and Imogen Blair's guest. I shuffled closer to Malachi as Marelaine took the spot on my left.

"What's Jean-Luc cooking?" I asked her.

She shrugged one shoulder. "Something French?"

Knowing Jean-Luc, he'd have talked about his dish constantly for the last week. She hadn't listened at all?

"Well, I'm sure it'll be delicious."

And it was, but the best part was still Malachi's

company. We each got a portion of Jean-Luc's spectacular croquembouche, and Malachi gave me most of his as well as finding me a glass of wine and feeding me more Advil. My hero. Today, I was the centre of his world, and I cherished that feeling. This was what I wanted, not the scraps Jean-Luc tossed my way. I'd always like him as a friend, but I'd come to realise he wasn't relationship material.

Still, I was thrilled when he won the contest along with the title of Virginia's best pastry chef. Marelaine didn't even attend the medal ceremony—she'd disappeared to the bathroom fifteen minutes earlier, and either she was still waiting in line or she'd gotten distracted.

"Want another glass of wine, babe?" Malachi asked once the official photos had been taken.

"I'd better not, but I'd love a glass of water."

He leaned down to kiss me on the cheek. "Back soon."

Jean-Luc watched him go. "Is it serious between you?"

"More serious than any other relationship I've been in."

That wasn't exactly a lie. Every other one of my relationships, if you could call them that, had been a disaster. At least I'd still want to speak to Malachi after today.

"Ah."

"Ah? What does *ah* mean?"

Jean-Luc fidgeted a bit, which wasn't like him. "I was just wondering whether you'd have dinner with me one day."

"Of course. We often have dinner."

"I meant in more of a date sort of way."

Oh. If he'd asked me that two weeks ago, I'd have jumped for joy, but now not only could I not jump because my legs still ached, I didn't want to go on a date with Jean-Luc either.

"What about Marelaine?"

"I think we've run our course."

"Does she know that?"

"I was planning on telling her this evening."

Jean-Luc trying to line me up before he split with his previous girlfriend just felt...sleazy. I'd definitely made the right decision, but I wanted to let him down gently because he was a friend. And that was all he'd ever be.

"I'm sorry it hasn't worked out for you two, but I don't think we're right for each other. So it's a no on the date, I'm afraid."

Jean-Luc shrugged, indifferent, so at least he had that in common with his soon-to-be ex. "Some you win, some you lose. I wish you all the happiness with Malachi. And I'll bring you over a box of pastries on Monday."

No hard feelings. Phew. Now I could focus on the future. My future. Malachi was right—I needed to stop pretending and put myself first. No more wild partying, no more hard drinking. I had some friends now, good friends, and they were worth more than the superficial relationships I'd gotten caught up with in the past. And I *was* a survivor. This week, I'd learned a lot about myself as well as getting through an attempted abduction, an actual abduction, and a fight. Was that some sort of record?

I smiled as Malachi came back, clutching a bottle of

water. Was it me, or did he look odd? Kind of wide-eyed?

"Are you okay?" Usually, that was his line.

"I am now I've escaped."

"Escaped from what?"

"Marelaine. She cornered me by the bar and propositioned me."

"*What*? Are you serious?"

"She fondled my cock, babe."

My first thought was holy hell, the woman had balls. Not Malachi's, luckily. My second thought? What a bitch.

"How dare she? I mean, that's low when you've got a girlfriend." *I wished.* "Well, a pretend girlfriend, but she doesn't know that."

"And she's got a boyfriend. I feel sorry for Jean-Luc."

"I wouldn't feel too bad for him. He's planning to dump her this evening."

"He told you that?"

"Yup, when he asked me out on a date."

"Fuck me, that pair deserves each other." Why had Malachi gone all stiff? "Uh, what did you say? About the date, I mean."

"I turned him down."

"Sorry it didn't work out, babe. I know you liked him."

"I've come to realise that he's better as a friend. I'll keep looking for the right man."

Speaking of looking, Malachi's gaze changed. His eyes darkened from their usual friendly twinkle to something more intense. Smouldering, even. And I was ninety-nine percent sure I recognised that expression because I wore it too. It said *I want you*. Holy freaking hell. Could I be right?

"Except... Except I think... I think I might have found him?"

Malachi didn't bother to answer, and the next thing I knew, he was half-carrying me out of the exhibition room. Suddenly, my legs didn't hurt anymore, and it wasn't due to the copious amounts of Advil I'd taken.

I stumbled, but Malachi didn't let me fall. I knew then that he'd never let me fall, but he did almost throw me into his car before jogging around to the driver's side.

"Babe."

That was it. One word and his lips were on mine. He kissed like a demon, fiery and dangerous, and I climbed halfway over the centre console to get as close to him as I could. My brain had barely processed what was happening, but Malachi Banks was mine and I was his. The rest we could work out later.

I lost track of time before we came up for air. All I knew was that my lips stung from stubble that was fast becoming a beard, and if we didn't get somewhere private quickly, then we'd both get arrested for public indecency. I already had my hands under his shirt, and the halterneck on my dress was undone.

Luckily, he seemed to have had the same idea because he lifted me back into my own seat and started the engine.

"Hold that thought, Miss Thomas."

Hearing my old name didn't hurt anymore, not when it came from his lips. It felt more like a secret we shared.

"Where are we going? Home?"

"My place. It's closer."

He'd barely mentioned anything about his house, but as long as it had a bed, it would be perfect.

"Drive faster."

"At least I brought the right car for that, babe."

CHAPTER 24 - IMOGEN

MALACHI SKIDDED THROUGH the electric gates into his driveway, and I got my first look at his place. Located on a quiet street on the outskirts of the city, it was bigger than I expected—two storeys with a two-car garage set at a right angle to the main house. The lot was mostly grass with a few trees, but the landscaping around the house was obsessively neat with potted flowers, perfectly edged borders, and not a weed or dead leaf in sight. I guess Malachi's experience in horticulture had paid off. And apart from one smaller home next door, the property wasn't overlooked by any other houses—privacy I'd only ever dreamed of.

But I didn't have time to gush over the manicured lawn or the wraparound porch or all the space because Malachi had the front door open.

"I'll give you the tour later." He paused in front of an electronic panel beside the front door. "Why's the security system off?"

"Maybe you forgot to set it?"

"I never forget to set it."

He changed from heady lust to strictly business in the blink of an eye, and a gun appeared in his hand. I didn't even see where it came from.

"Stay behind me."

It was fate, wasn't it? Conspiring against me—us—

as we tried to finally plug that person-sized gap in our lives. Or what if it was Kyle? On my own, I would have been terrified, but Malachi was so calm, so confident, I managed not to freeze.

We crept through the house, pausing to check one room after another. My heartbeat was loud in my ears, and each time we moved on, my knees quaked harder. Malachi reached back with his free hand, and I clutched at it. He gave me a comforting squeeze.

"Don't worry, babe. I've got this."

Breathe, Imogen. Just breathe. Don't think about dying. I tried to focus on the decor instead. Malachi seemed to be a fan of monochrome—almost everything was black, white, or grey—and it wasn't until we reached the master bedroom upstairs that we found a splash of colour.

"What the fuck are you doing here?" he growled.

Erin lay on the bed, wearing a nightie skimpier than any of mine and a dirty smile.

"Waiting for you. What's *she* doing here?"

"What, do you need a fucking biology lesson? How did you get in?"

"With my key."

"I took your key back."

"I had a spare made in case I lost it."

"Get out."

"You don't mean that."

Malachi rolled his eyes to the ceiling. "Yes, I definitely do mean that."

"Why do you keep messing around with that woman? If you're trying to make me jealous, it isn't working. I'm worth ten of her."

"You're delusional."

"No, I'm just honest."

She also knew how to get her digs in where it hurt the most. I'd never be a model like her, all long legs and huge hair. Mom always said I'd never amount to much, and I hadn't even gotten my high school diploma.

Malachi moved fast. In a second, he'd picked up Erin, arms around her waist as she turned into the bitch I'd met in Florida. Her limbs flailed as she kicked and screamed.

"Imogen, get the front door."

I hurried ahead down the stairs, fingers trembling as they fumbled at the lock. After what seemed like forever, I yanked the door open, but Erin managed to grab onto my dress as Malachi carried her past, clawing and tearing at the fabric as she wailed. By the time he got her outside, the beautiful silk looked more like a Halloween costume, and my heart was threatening to hammer through my ribcage. Even then, she didn't give up, and her arms snaked around the door like a zombie in a horror movie. I unpeeled her fingers from the doorjamb as Malachi muttered curses under his breath.

"Doesn't this psycho ever give up?"

The door finally closed with a click, and I sagged against it with relief, only for the crash of broken glass to come from the next room. Malachi hastily punched commands into the security system, and the house turned dark as metal shutters rolled down over the windows.

He crouched beside me where I'd slithered to the floor. "Babe, I'm so sorry. Are you okay?"

"Her nails didn't break the skin this time."

"That wasn't what I meant."

"I'm fine."

He gathered me up in his arms, and tears prickled at the corners of my eyes.

"Stop pretending, Imogen," he murmured.

A sniffle escaped before I could stop it. "No, I'm not okay."

Banging came from outside as Erin threw whatever she could get her hands on at the house. It sounded like bricks.

"Shit. Let me fix this."

He helped me to my feet and clicked on all the lights as he led me through to a study on the first floor. Monitors on one wall showed Erin beating the hell out of the shutter over the front door with one of the metal flower pots that had decorated the front porch.

"Now what? Should we go out there?"

"No way. She wants my attention, and if she gets it, she wins. Don't worry; I have favours owing." He pulled his phone out of his pants pocket and spoke softly into it. "I need a car at my house. Erin's lost her mind, and she's trying to break in. I'm inside with Imogen... Yeah... Yeah... Somewhere far, far away."

I didn't hear the other side of the conversation, but when Malachi hung up, he glanced at his watch.

"Fifteen minutes and she'll be gone." His phone rang, and he checked the screen and answered. "Yeah, I know, buddy. Thanks. Someone's on their way to deal with it." This time, he smiled as he stuffed the phone back into his pocket. "That was Deon, calling to tell me Erin's trying to break in. His bedroom window overlooks the garden, and he keeps an eye on things."

"Shame he didn't see her arriving in the first place."

"Yeah, it is. Fuck." Malachi sucked in a deep breath. "I should've changed the locks."

"You couldn't have known she'd do this."

"I should've guessed. She's totally unhinged."

"Besides, you were too busy changing *my* lock, which was so freaking sweet." I'd lost my shoes somewhere in the struggle, so I stood on tiptoes to kiss him on the lips. "*You're* so freaking sweet."

He kissed me back, properly with tongues, and I'd even started to enjoy it when a loud bang made me jump. A glance at the monitors told me Erin and her dented plant pot had moved around the house.

And now she started screaming. "She's a whore, Malachi!"

Another jab right between the ribs.

"Don't listen to her. She's a raving lunatic."

He lifted me into his arms, bridal style, and carried me upstairs where it was quieter. A pile of Erin's clothes still lay on a chair beside his bed, and he raised one shutter high enough to drop them out of the window. I threw her pumps out too.

"Talk to me, babe."

At first, I wasn't sure what to say, but I'd promised to stop pretending.

"I'm scared." When I held out a hand, it was still shaking. "Scared of everything. Of Erin. Of being on my own. Of doing something wrong and screwing up possibly the best thing ever to happen to me."

Malachi kissed my forehead. "I'm scared too."

"You? Scared of what?"

"Of losing you. I get we haven't known each other for long, but I'm already in deep."

"Well, not yet. Erin interrupted us."

That thing about laughter being the best medicine? It was true. Malachi looked at me, I giggled, and then we both doubled over.

"If we can get through this past week..." I snorted, which was horrifying, but Malachi only laughed harder. "We can get through anything."

"Insane exes, stalkers with eyesight problems, assholes at the gym..."

"Ohmigosh! I forgot to say—Lisa heard about a guy getting a sheep tattooed on his face, and I was wondering...?"

"It was a pig. Emmy can't draw to save her life."

Tears rolled down my cheeks, except this time they were all good. Malachi still wiped them away with his thumbs.

"No crying in the bedroom. That's my rule. Unless you're weeping with shock over my size—then I might make an exception."

Was that an invitation? It sounded like an invitation. Years of practice meant I got his belt buckle open faster than he could draw his gun, and oh my... He was big *everywhere*.

"You might as well shred the rest of the dress," I told him. "Have at it."

One good tug and it was gone. At least it wasn't the favourite little blue number I'd originally wanted to wear to the contest. I was still a few pounds off fitting into that again, but judging by Malachi's low whistle, he didn't care.

"Tell me you always wear this shit."

"Fancy underwear? It's kind of my thing. Even if I'm plain on the surface, I like to feel pretty underneath."

"Miss Thomas, you'll never be plain. But please, abuse my credit card and buy as much of this stuff as you want because I want to peel it off you every night."

"Every night? So you want to become my new roommate?"

"Maybe... I figured you could just move in here when you're ready."

Was he joking around with me? "Here? Into your monochrome palace?"

"Redecorate it. I don't care." A quick fumble and my bra ended up on the floor. He squeezed my boobs together and grinned. "Now I can stare at these all day without risk of you slapping me."

"You might want to look at my face occasionally too. It's only polite."

He came in for a kiss, deep and slow, pausing to suck on my bottom lip and give it a nibble. Yes, I liked bedroom Malachi already. Bedroom Malachi was fun, and that was a whole new experience for me. I gave a little hop and wrapped my legs around his waist. My thighs were sticky, and that fact didn't escape his notice.

"You're wet as fuck, babe."

"I'm also impatient as fuck. So hurry the fuck up and fuck me."

"I love that mouth on you."

"I can do more than curse with it."

He fell back onto the bed with me sitting on top of him, cowgirl style.

"Dead. I'm dead."

"What happened to your stamina? Once your muscles build up..." I mimicked.

"One second." He reached behind him to the nightstand and grabbed a handful of condoms out of the drawer. "Take your pick."

Flavoured, ribbed, glow in the freaking dark... Rather than dwell on why the hell he had all those, I thought positive—I was truly spoiled. But I picked out an extra-sensitive because I wanted him to enjoy this too. He groaned when I rolled it on, and when I lowered myself on top of him, he let out a long exhale then offered me his hands to steady myself.

This. This was what I'd always wanted. A real partner, not just in the bedroom but everywhere else too. And I'd found him. I'd finally found him.

Waking up in Malachi's house was different than waking up in my apartment. Not just because of the king-sized bed and the warm body wrapped around me, but because of the silence. At home, there was traffic even early in the morning, and before my upstairs neighbour had started trying to deafen us all, there'd been footsteps and voices in the hallway. Here, there was birdsong.

The peace gave me time to think, and by the time Malachi stirred, I had two questions I needed to know the answers to.

"You're still here," he mumbled, his arms tightening.

"Of course I'm still here. You thought I'd leave?"

"Couldn't blame you after yesterday."

Which brought me to my first question...

"What happened to Erin?"

It had gone blessedly quiet, and thanks to Malachi's distractions, I'd temporarily forgotten about her.

"No idea. Want to find out?"

"Honestly? I'm not sure."

"Better the devil you know."

Malachi found his phone and dialled, and it only took a moment for somebody to pick up.

"Lemme guess—you want to know what happened to Looney Tunes?"

Emmy sounded kind of sleepy.

"Imogen's here, and you're on speaker."

"Imogen's there? At six a.m.? Then that means... Oh, fuck. Luther won the pool again. We should start renting him out as a psychic. Uh, congratulations."

"Thanks. Where's Erin?"

"Right now? I'm not totally sure. We dropped her off in Kentucky."

"What do you mean, dropped her off? And who's 'we'?"

"Me and Fia. We left her at the side of a road."

"What? Just left her there?" I asked. "In that negligée she was wearing?"

"Bet it didn't take long for her to hitch a ride."

"Oh my goodness."

"Hey, it wasn't that bad. She had her purse. Well, sort of. Fia emptied the contents over a half-mile stretch then chucked her clutch into a bush. It probably took her a while to gather everything up."

Perhaps I should've felt guilty since I knew how horrible it was to be abandoned alone on the side of a road, but I couldn't bring myself to care. In fact, the thought of that banshee trying to walk back to Virginia in four-inch pumps brought a smile to my face. After all her antics, Erin deserved everything she got.

"Do you think she'll come back?"

"I told her that every time she got within a hundred

yards of you or Mal, we'd collect her and drop her one state farther west. Unless she wants to end up in the Pacific, she'll quit while she's ahead."

"Thank you. For everything."

"Just make him happy, yeah?"

Then she was gone, and I took her advice to heart. Thanks to my former career, I knew how to take a man right past happy and all the way to delirious, only now it was pleasurable for both of us and not just for him.

Afterwards, Mal lay spread-eagled on the bed.

"Going to the gym every day in no way prepared me for meeting you. Those jaw muscles are something else."

"Then you'll just have to practise every day until it becomes second nature."

"I'll have to go to the office for a rest. Are you working today?"

"Ten until five thirty. You?"

"I can work around that. Where are we staying tonight? Here or your place?"

My second question... "I was thinking about that. Were you serious about me moving in one day? I don't want to sound pushy or anything. It's just that if I only need my apartment for a few more months, I might be able to get by without a roommate. Apart from Stef, I always seem to end up with crazies, and if I can be on my own then—"

Malachi pressed a finger to my lips. "Given the choice, I'd have you living here by the weekend."

Did I hear that right? "Like, this weekend?"

"Too soon?"

"I'm just... I never..."

"Give it some thought. I'm ready whenever you are,

but there's no hurry."

"So no roommate?"

"No roommate. I'll help out with the rent if you need it. But you're still getting an alarm system."

Was a day after your first semi-official date too soon to tell a man you loved him? Because I did. I loved Malachi. I loved everything about him. The first half of my life might have been a crazy ride, but now I'd arrived at my destination, and I'd spend the rest of my time exploring everything it had to offer.

Finally, I felt complete.

Epilogue - Imogen

TWO MONTHS. IT took me two months to abandon any pretence of living in my apartment and hand the keys back. Which was longer than the three weeks it took for me to tell Malachi I loved him. Luckily, he'd said it right back, that day and every day since.

For the first month, I'd been terrified Erin would make a reappearance despite Emmy's assurances, but then Malachi heard on the grapevine that she'd gotten married. Married! Apparently, she'd pledged her eternal love to some poor schmuck who picked her up at the side of the road in her underwear, a schmuck who just happened to have a healthy trust fund. Goodness knows what sob story she'd spun him, but she was out of our hair, and for that, I had to be thankful. Malachi gave them three months, max.

The second month, I'd had a crisis of confidence that this was all too good to be true. I'd got everything I'd always wanted, and the part of me that used to quake under the covers at night as I listened for Kyle was terrified I'd wake up and find myself back in a nightmare. But Malachi knew something was wrong, and he had a way of drawing the darkness out of me and replacing it with light. He reassured me this was real. That he was real. That *we* were real.

Tonight, he was working late, which meant I could

organise my first ever girls' night in my new home. A home I adored. Malachi had given me free rein with the decor, although so far, I'd only managed to buy a rug for the bedroom, a pair of sun loungers, and a new cookie jar. It was too cold to sit outside now, but I loved having so much space. On weekends, I helped Malachi to get the garden ready for winter, pruning shrubs and carrying the more delicate potted plants into the greenhouse. In the evenings, I was teaching myself to cook properly, and of course, there were plenty of fresh herbs. We even had a compost bin. Niles would've been proud.

As I'd feared, I didn't sleep well when Malachi was away on a job, especially when he couldn't tell me what was going on, but I was learning to cope. The Blackwood control room was only at the end of the phone, and they didn't mind if I called for reassurance, day or night. And now that I'd seen Malachi in action first-hand, I knew he could look after himself.

Roxy and Stef were on their way over, pizza was being delivered, and Jean-Luc had donated pastries. I'd had a lucky escape there—he was already on his second girlfriend since Marelaine, and yesterday, he'd complained she was getting too clingy.

My phone chirped to let me know a car was at the gates, and when I checked the app, I saw it was Roxy's Audi and buzzed her in. Now that I was living there, Malachi had overhauled the entire security system because he wanted me to be safe. I thought that was a bit drastic, but Stef and Roxy assured me that Oliver and Gideon had done exactly the same thing when they got together.

Roxy parked next to my car and hopped out with

Stef. Yes, my car. Malachi had bought it for me since I was learning to drive. He refused to let me repay him, the same way as he refused to take any rent money. Despite being only two years older than me, he owned the house free and clear and told me to buy myself more underwear with the money I saved instead.

"Hey, I brought wine," Stef said, squeezing me tightly. "And candles. The candles are actually from Bradley, and he says he's going to bring over throw pillows this weekend. I'm not sure whether you'll want to warn Malachi or not."

"He won't mind."

"Lucky you. Oliver's started dropping them down the trash chute now."

Roxy tried to hug me too, but it was difficult with the huge bouquet of flowers she was carrying.

"I accidentally let slip to Gideon that we planned on doing face masks, so he sent three thousand dollars' worth of spa vouchers. Basically, we've all got to get a massage every month for the next year. Sorry."

"I think I can live with that."

"What are we watching?" Stef asked. "An old classic?"

"Nope, because you've seen them all. Tonight..." I gestured towards the living room, where bowls of popcorn awaited. "Tonight, I give you the new Scott Lowes movie. It's set on a tropical island, and he takes his shirt off a lot."

I could still look, okay?

"Does he have a suntan?" Roxy asked. "Tell me he has a suntan. I had to watch three autopsies today, and there's only so much pasty skin a girl can take."

"He has a suntan. And a six-pack. Stef, do you need

a corkscrew?"

"I came prepared. We just need three wine glasses."

I'd missed the girls. Between me meeting Malachi and moving house, Stef having a baby, and Roxy's new job at the hospital, we hadn't seen enough of each other. But that could change now. Life had finally settled down.

And I was happy.

Relaxed.

At least, I was until my phone rang during the closing credits. My back stiffened automatically when I saw it was a Cleveland number. Who the hell was calling me from Cleveland?

"Hello?"

"Miss Thomas?" a woman said.

"Who's asking?"

"This is Detective Marquette with the Cleveland PD Bureau of Special Investigations."

I gripped the phone harder. "What do you want?"

"Is this Imogen Thomas?"

"Yes."

"I'm afraid I have some... Well, I'd normally say bad news, but I've been reading through the complaint you filed a decade ago, and I'm not so sure. I'm afraid Kyle Thomas has been found deceased. I believe he's your brother?"

"What?"

"It happened a week ago, but he's only just been identified. We had his prints on file from an old shoplifting charge. I'm afraid he took his own life."

"How?"

"A single gunshot wound to the head."

"Are you sure? That it's him, I mean."

"My colleagues in Michigan assure me there's no mistake. They've closed the case, but there's still the body to consider."

"What's that got to do with me?"

"Do you want to claim it?"

"You said you read my file?"

"Yes."

"Then you already know the answer to that. Try calling my mother."

"From what I understand, she's hospitalised for a heart condition at the moment."

"Then I guess he'll just have to rot." I screwed my eyes shut for a second. "Sorry. I'm not trying to be awkward. I just don't want anything more to do with either of them."

"I can appreciate that. Is there any other assistance I can offer?"

"No, nothing. Have a good day."

I hung up, breathing hard. Stef and Roxy stared at me.

"Was that what I think it was?" Stef asked.

"If you think my brother's dead, then yes."

"That's, uh, good news?"

My response was to walk to the fridge in the kitchen. Emmy had given us a bottle of champagne as a housewarming gift, and we'd decided to save it for a special celebration. Tonight was that occasion. Malachi would understand.

In the living room, I popped the cork, and it ricocheted off a piece of black-and-white abstract art Malachi had confessed to buying on the internet while drunk.

"Yes, it's good news."

"How did he die? I hope it was painful."

"He shot himself."

"Suicide?"

"That's what the police said."

But I knew differently. Kyle was far too arrogant to have taken his own life. He'd had help, help from someone far smarter and more cunning than he was. I allowed myself a small smile.

Stef had scored gold, Roxy ended up with platinum, and I'd gotten lead, but I knew now that I was the winner. Lead was an anchor, keeping me grounded in a world that veered from scary to chaotic at times. Lead was a shield protecting me from hurt. And finally, lead was a bullet, an efficient way of cutting the cancer out of my life.

Malachi was my lead, and I wouldn't change him for anything.

WHAT'S NEXT?

The Blackwood Elements series continues in
Copper...

When Tai Beaulieu impulsively hands in her notice by
text message one dreary January morning and sets off
in search of adventure, the last place she expects to end
up is Africa. But soon she's in Egypt, home to ancient
tombs and spectacular temples. Plus friendly locals, a
rather nice English businessman and, an American
tourist who doesn't know when to butt out.

Along with roommate Tegan and archaeologist
Miles, Tai sets out to explore everything the city of
Luxor has to offer. But soon, she's keeping a terrible
secret, and she's not the only one.

For more details: www.elise-noble.com/copper

Want to find out more about Emmy? Her story starts in *Pitch Black*...

What happens when an assassin has a nervous breakdown?

After the owner of a security company is murdered, his sharp-edged wife goes on the run. Forced to abandon everything she holds dear—her home, her friends, her job in special ops—she builds a new life for herself in England. As Ashlyn Hale, she meets Luke, a handsome local who makes her realise just how lonely she is.

Yet, even in the sleepy village of Lower Foxford, the dark side of life dogs Diamond's trail when the unthinkable strikes. Forced out of hiding, she races against time to save those she cares about. But is it too little, too late?

Pitch Black is currently available FREE.
For more details: www.elise-noble.com/pitch-black

If you enjoyed *Lead*, please consider leaving a review.

For an author, every review is incredibly important. Not only do they make us feel warm and fuzzy inside, readers consider them when making their decision whether or not to buy a book. Even a line saying you enjoyed the book or what your favourite part was helps a lot.

Want to Stalk Me?

For updates on my new releases, giveaways, and
other random stuff, you can sign up for my newsletter
on my website:
www.elise-noble.com

Facebook:
www.facebook.com/EliseNobleAuthor

Twitter: @EliseANoble

Instagram: @elise_noble

If you're on social media, you may also like to join
Team Blackwood for exclusive giveaways, sneak
previews, and book-related chat. Be the first to find out
about new stories, and you might even see your name
or one of your ideas make it into print!

And if you'd like to read my books for FREE, you
can also find details of how to join my review team.

Would you like to join Team Blackwood?

www.elise-noble.com/team-blackwood

End-of-Book Stuff

Originally, I planned to write a little novella for Imogen because I felt kind of bad that Stef and Roxy had got their happy endings and she was still single. But she and Malachi turned out to be more complex than I ever thought they would be, then Morton Seacroft schlepped in, Emmy got involved, and Lead became a novel. A novel about second chances. Most people deserve a second chance, and if somebody makes the effort to change their life for the better, then a helping hand can work wonders.

The "bad dates" thing was inspired by a Twitter post. I'm guilty of wasting far too much time on there when I should be working, but for once, it paid off. A guy listed the overly intrusive questions he asked girls on a first date to weed out those he felt were unworthy, and the general consensus was "what a dick." So I thought it would be fun to have Imogen have dinner with a man just like him. Plus a bunch of other assholes before someone took pity and set her up with Malachi.

And Storm turned up again. She's not even supposed to be in this series right now, but she and Emmy seem to get on quite well so I figured I'd let her have a few words, lol. She'll be back later in the Blackstone House saga.

I'm writing this in the middle of February, and by

the time you read it, Britain will have Brexited. Or not, who knows? I rarely comment on politics, but honestly, what a bloody mess everything is right now. Nobody seems to know what's going on, least of all the people in charge. It's times like this I'm really happy I've got a fictional world to escape into! My TBR list is long, and I'm off to stock up on hot chocolate, yoga pants, and possibly a beanbag chair.

See you on the other side!

Elise

Huge thanks to everyone who assisted with this novel: Amanda for editing, Abi for designing the cover, and Lizbeth, John, Debi, and Dominique for proof reading. Plus my team of awesome beta readers—Jeff, Renata, Terri, Lina, Must, David, Stacia, Jessica, Nikita, Quenby, and Jody. You guys rock!

OTHER BOOKS BY ELISE NOBLE

The Blackwood Security Series

For the Love of Animals (Nate & Carmen - prequel)
Black is My Heart (Diamond & Snow - prequel)
Pitch Black
Into the Black
Forever Black
Gold Rush
Gray is My Heart
Neon (novella)
Out of the Blue
Ultraviolet
Glitter (novella)
Red Alert
White Hot
Sphere (novella)
The Scarlet Affair
Spirit (novella)
Quicksilver
The Girl with the Emerald Ring
Red After Dark
When the Shadows Fall
Pretties in Pink (TBA)

The Blackwood Elements Series
Oxygen

Lithium
Carbon
Rhodium
Platinum
Lead
Copper
Bronze
Nickel
Hydrogen (2021)

The Blackwood UK Series
Joker in the Pack
Cherry on Top (novella)
Roses are Dead
Shallow Graves
Indigo Rain
Pass the Parcel (TBA)

Baldwin's Shore
Dirty Little Secrets (2021)
Secrets, Lies, and Family Ties (2021)
Buried Secrets (2021)

Blackwood Casefiles
Stolen Hearts
Burning Love (TBA)

Blackstone House
Hard Lines (TBA)
Hard Tide (TBA)

The Electi Series
Cursed

Spooked
Possessed
Demented
Judged

The Planes Series
A Vampire in Vegas
A Devil in the Dark (TBA)

The Trouble Series
Trouble in Paradise
Nothing but Trouble
24 Hours of Trouble

Standalone
Life
Coco du Ciel (2021)
Twisted (short stories)
A Very Happy Christmas (novella)

Books with clean versions available (no swearing and no on-the-page sex)
Pitch Black
Into the Black
Forever Black
Gold Rush
Gray is My Heart

Audiobooks
Black is My Heart (Diamond & Snow - prequel)
Pitch Black
Into the Black
Forever Black

Gold Rush
Gray is My Heart
Neon (novella)

Made in the USA
Las Vegas, NV
31 March 2022

46649415R00132